WATCH ME

bestselling authors
KER DUKEY & K WEBSTER

Watch Me

Copyright © 2019 Ker Dukey
Copyright © 2019 K Webster

Cover Design: All by Design
Photo: Adobe Stock
Editor: Word Nerd Editing
Formatting: Champagne Book Design

ALL RIGHTS RESERVED. This book contains material protected under International and Federal Copyright Laws and Treaties. Any unauthorized reprint or use of this material is prohibited. No part of this book may be reproduced or transmitted in any form or by any means, electronic or mechanical, including photocopying, recording, or by an information and retrieval system without express written permission from the Author/Publisher.

This is a work of fiction. Names, characters, places, and incidents either are the product of the author's imagination or are used fictitiously, and any resemblance to actual persons, living or dead, business establishments, events, or locales is entirely coincidental.

From international bestselling authors, **Ker Dukey and K Webster**, *comes a **fast-paced**, hot, **insta-love** standalone **lunchtime read** from their KKinky Reads collection!*

I like to watch.

It's a compulsion I can't stop.
Now, my desire is centered around one woman.
My obsession borders on stalking, but the glass wall keeps me in check.

She can't see my face, yet she dances in an intensely erotic and intimate way that feels designed just for me.
She likes when I watch her.

But things are about to change when she waltzes out of that room and into my tattoo parlor, turning my world completely upside down.

There's no glass wall this time.

*This is a steamy, kinky romance sure to make you blush! A perfect combination of sweet and sexy you can **devour in one sitting**! You'll get a **happy ending** that'll make you swoon!*

This is not a dark romance.

BOOKS BY
KER DUKEY

Empathy Series:
Empathy
Desolate
Vacant—Novella
Deadly—Novella

The Broken Series:
The Broken
The Broken Parts of Us
The Broken Tethers That Bind Us—Novella
The Broken Forever—Novella

The Men by Numbers Series:
Ten
Six

Drawn to You Duet:
Drawn to You
Lines Drawn

Standalone Novels:
My Soul Keeper
Lost
I See You
The Beats in Rift
Devil

Co-Written with D. Sidebottom

The Deception Series:
FaCade
Cadence

Beneath Innocence—Novella

The Lilith's Army MC Series:
Taking Avery
Finding Rhiannon
Coming Home TBA

Co-Written with K Webster

The Pretty Little Dolls Series:
Pretty Stolen Dolls
Pretty Lost Dolls
Pretty New Doll
Pretty Broken Dolls

The V Games Series:
Vlad
Ven
Vas

KKinky Reads Collection:
Share Me
Choke Me
Daddy Me
Watch Me

Joint Series

Four Fathers Series:
Blackstone by J.D. Hollyfield
Kingston by Dani René
Pearson by K Webster
Wheeler by Ker Dukey

Four Sons Series:
Nixon by Ker Dukey
Hayden by J.D Hollyfield
Brock by Dani René
Camden by K Webster

The Elite Seven Series:
Lust—Ker Dukey
Pride—J.D. Hollyfield
Wrath—Claire C. Riley
Envy—M.N.Forgy
Gluttony—K Webster
Sloth—Giana Darling
Greed—Ker Dukey & K Webster

BOOKS BY K WEBSTER

Psychological Romance Standalones:
My Torin
Whispers and the Roars
Cold Cole Heart
Blue Hill Blood

Romantic Suspense Standalones:
Dirty Ugly Toy
El Malo
Notice
Sweet Jayne
The Road Back to Us
Surviving Harley
Love and Law
Moth to a Flame
Erased

Extremely Forbidden Romance Standalones:
The Wild
Hale
Like Dragonflies

Taboo Treats:
Bad Bad Bad
Coach Long
Ex-Rated Attraction
Mr. Blakely
Easton
Crybaby
Lawn Boys
Malfeasance
Renner's Rules
The Glue
Dane
Enzo
Red Hot Winter

KKinky Reads Collection:
Share Me
Choke Me
Daddy Me
Watch Me

Contemporary Romance Standalones:
The Day She Cried
Untimely You
Heath
Sundays are for Hangovers
A Merry Christmas with Judy
Zeke's Eden
Schooled by a Senior
Give Me Yesterday
Sunshine and the Stalker
Bidding for Keeps
B-Sides and Rarities

Paranormal Romance Standalones:
Apartment 2B
Running Free
Mad Sea

War & Peace Series:
This is War, Baby (Book 1)
This is Love, Baby (Book 2)
This Isn't Over, Baby (Book 3)
This Isn't You, Baby (Book 4)
This is Me, Baby (Book 5)
This Isn't Fair, Baby (Book 6)
This is the End, Baby (Book 7—a novella)

Lost Planet Series:
The Forgotten Commander (Book 1)
The Vanished Specialist (Book 2)
The Mad Lieutenant (Book 3)

2 Lovers Series:
Text 2 Lovers (Book 1)
Hate 2 Lovers (Book 2)
Thieves 2 Lovers (Book 3)

Pretty Little Dolls Series:
Pretty Stolen Dolls (Book 1)
Pretty Lost Dolls (Book 2)
Pretty New Doll (Book 3)
Pretty Broken Dolls (Book 4)

The V Games Series:
Vlad (Book 1)
Ven (Book 2)
Vas (Book 3)

Four Fathers Books:
Pearson

Four Sons Books:
Camden

Elite Seven Books:
Gluttony

Not Safe for Amazon Books:
The Wild
Hale
Bad Bad Bad
This is War, Baby
Like Dragonflies

The Breaking the Rules Series:
Broken (Book 1)
Wrong (Book 2)
Scarred (Book 3)
Mistake (Book 4)
Crushed (Book 5—a novella)

The Vegas Aces Series:
Rock Country (Book 1)
Rock Heart (Book 2)
Rock Bottom (Book 3)

The Becoming Her Series:
Becoming Lady Thomas (Book 1)
Becoming Countess Dumont (Book 2)
Becoming Mrs. Benedict (Book 3)

Alpha & Omega Duet:
Alpha & Omega (Book 1)
Omega & Love (Book 2)

For those who like to watch

WATCH me

PROLOGUE

Lucca

This club makes my bar look tired and dated. All the time I shot down my sister's ideas to make the bar better, more current, and it turns out she was right. This place is packed and buzzing with a contagious energy. I never wanted that fucking bar in the first place. I know our dad left it to me because he thought he was giving me a future, but in reality, it just took the future I had planned for myself away. And now, the whole reason I even accepted the bar in the first place, is flying off to better things. With this prick sitting across from me with his fancy watch and expensive whisky. My baby sister wants to be famous and this asshole has all the means to make that happen.

"She's too young." My argument is weak and I know it. But I won't let this fucking asshole take my sister without a fight. She's all I have left. Some record exec in a fancy suit and gelled hair can't swoop in, wave money in her face, and drag her away from me. I've given up everything for Sofina. Fucking everything.

I glower at Ronan Hayes—CEO of Harose Records—my fists tightening with the urge to pummel his smug face. It was already infuriating for him to invite me here in the first place. To have to tell the doorman out front of this club that I was his guest. I know he's into those power trips and I'll be damned if I show him one ounce of gratitude. I'm here because of one reason.

Sofina.

"To know she's in love?" he probes, his eyes hard and calculating. "To know her own mind and make her own choices? How old were you when you fell in love?"

My chest aches at his words. Too young. Too stupid.

"It's different."

His nostrils flare. "Why? Because she's your

sister?" He rolls his eyes and checks his watch as though this very conversation bores him. "We're not that different, you and I," he continues, piercing me with his authoritative stare. "My mother died, and I had to be the man, take care of my younger brother, and step up. But you need to know. You did your job. She's grown. She's starting her career and her life."

Sadness and loss roil around inside me. Mom left us when we were young. It was just me, Dad, and Sof. When Dad died, then it was just the two of us. I hate that she'll be gone soon too. Then what happens to me? Why does everyone I fucking care about leave me?

"I don't know who I am without her," I admit, bowing my head and running my fingers through my hair. "She's all I've got." It's the fucking truth. I gave up everything else to be here for her. To raise her.

"Then don't lose her by giving ultimatums and expecting her to choose a mediocre life. It's beneath her. She's too talented, Lucca. Don't darken her dreams by making her live them without you."

Another ache in my chest. I can't lose her. Not over this. Anger surges through me. We wouldn't even be having this conversation if this asshole didn't show up on his white horse thinking he needed to save her from the person who loves her the most in this world.

"Why do you care? Why did you call me here?" I demand. He must have an agenda.

"Because she misses you. I see her hurting, and it pains me to see her in distress."

"You act like you love her."

"I do love her."

His words are a sucker punch to my gut. Love hurts. It hurts really fucking badly. I know because love sliced me open and left me bleeding years ago. I'm still bleeding, dammit.

"You want my approval and for me to let you have her." That's not going to fucking happen.

"She's already mine, Lucca. I'm not asking for anything. I'm giving you the chance to stop being a dick and give your sister what she actually needs."

The nerve of this prick. "And what's that?"

"You. Your support and love."

Our conversation is silenced when someone announces my sister's name on the microphone, booming and loud. It cannot be ignored. Ronan has my sister, and now everyone else will too. I'm losing her. What will I do now that she doesn't need me anymore?

Who the fuck am I without her without the burden I've always felt on my shoulders to run the bar, to take care of the house, to take care of her—of us?

I'm lost in my thoughts when someone sits beside me as Ronan's guest. I glance up to a woman I've seen more times than I'd like to admit.

Nina.

My dick twitches in recognition.

Twilight Nina from Boondock's—a strip joint I often frequent.

Often is an understatement. All my free time is spent watching the women there, but never able to bring myself to touch. It's safer that way. When you finally latch on, they'll pry themselves loose and leave you broken. I know from experience. So Nina, and all the other women at Boondock's, get my undivided attention and wads of cash, but that's all they'll ever get.

"I know you from somewhere, right?" I ask, letting Ronan know I fucking know the company he's keeping is a stripper. I've fucked my fist to Nina's face a few times in the safety of my bedroom.

She blushes and shakes her head in vehemence. "No, I don't think so."

Nina wants to keep her secrets and I want to keep mine. When I nod at her, to let her know I'm not going to make shit awkward by announcing where I know her from, she lets out a breath of relief. Ronan watches me with narrowed eyes. By letting him know I know her, I've given him a tad bit of information on me, but there's no way he has any idea how fucked in the head I am. I'm barely trying to understand it myself.

Ignoring them both for now, I turn my attention to the stage. My sister—sweet, little Sofina—is all grown up and flapping her wings. I've raised her, but it looks like her time to fly is now, and I'll be left in the nest all alone.

Her beautiful voice belts through the speakers sending a chill down my spine. She owns the stage, the audience. Fuck, and judging by the way Ronan's puppy dog eyes drinking her in, it's clear she owns him too, not the other way around. Maybe I've been looking at this all wrong. Maybe she's not leaving me… maybe she's setting me free—setting us both free. If Sofina can go after her dreams, maybe I can too. My mind drifts back to my college days when I was happy and in love. I could always go back. Start over. Find me. As Sofina sings, for the first time in years, a tiny seed of hope grows inside me.

•••••▬•••••

I tried to stay away, but I can't. It's not like I'm getting laid. Not that I can't, it's just I don't want to. No one ever measures up to perfection. When I watch, they remain perfect as they can be. I don't hear their voice that'll be all wrong. I don't kiss them knowing they don't kiss like *her*. I don't fuck them wishing they were someone else. Watching is safe.

Nina isn't here tonight and I'm glad. Another girl named Fiona wriggles her ass on the stage and I stare at her from afar. Countless guys throw money at her and she lets a few of them tuck the bills into her G-string.

Not me.

I usually set a handful of bills at their feet before I walk away in shame.

I nod my head when a blonde asks if I want a private dance.

Creeping through the club to the backroom, I

watch her nice ass jiggle in booty shorts a size too small. I let her lead me into a dark room and to a red leather seat in the shape of a half-moon anchored around a pole.

"You want lap or pole?" she purrs.

"Don't speak or touch me. Dance like it's for you," I order, taking a seat. "Show me how much you love yourself. Pretend I'm not here."

She shrugs her petite shoulders and climbs up on the pole. It's fucking crazy the way they can move their bodies, like a snake around its prey. Twisting and contorting like a gymnast.

She's pretty in a cute way—pale skin like porcelain, big blue eyes, doll like features, and natural tits that bounce with her movements.

Playing the game I started, her eyes never stray to me. Instead, she looks down at herself, admiring and touching like a good girl.

My chest lifts with labored breathing as my urges react to watching her. Seeing her so involved and in tune with her own body has the blood rushing to my cock. She's bending and curling around the pole like it's part of her, while slipping a hand over her flesh, groping and getting lost to the pleasure of her touch.

Pushing down her shorts, she reveals a bare, thick-lipped pussy—a tattoo on her mound flutters with her movements. It's of a butterfly. A smirk tugs up my lips, and then memories of designing and getting my first ink propels me from the moment, before plunging me into guilt. Self hatred and regret.

Who have I become?

Watching a life from afar, but never participating.

I need a change of scenery. I'm getting the hell out of this town and going back to a place that stole so much from me.

I'm going to steal a little bit of it back.

Fucking watch me.

1

Lucca

Seven months later...

Controlled chaos is what I love most about living in the city.

Everyone rushing around, going to their jobs—homes—hobbies. Taxi drivers honking at each other in traffic. The hustler on every corner selling some knock-off shit no one needs.

It's calming, in a fucked up way.

Only in a city like Boston can you be surrounded by people, but feel alone in your own space. Your own thoughts. People mind their own fucking business, and everyone has a different reason for being here. It's freeing in a sense.

Six years, I've been away from this place, yet it feels the same as it always has.

My mind unwillingly drifts to *her* again. *Autumn fucking Jenkins.*

Who names their kid after a fucking season? I wish I could erase the fucking name from my brain. The memories of the woman who took my heart, put it in a blender, poured herself a nice full glass, and drank that shit down won't stop haunting me—the vengeful spirit of a woman who isn't even dead.

She's dead to you.

A light rain dusts the road in a sheen of mist. I pick up my pace before it becomes a full-on torrent.

The club lights illuminate the sign like a beacon for the depraved.

TEASE! TEASE! TEASE! EXOTIC DANCERS!

"Come inside and let us take care of you."

Entering the club is like coming home. I spend more time at this fucking place than my own. It's not something I share with anyone. My need to watch allows me to feel highs I don't get from anything else. It's a compulsion more than anything. I'm an addict. I don't medicate with drugs. This is my remedy for feeling anything other than angry. Dark. Alone.

Before moving back a little over six months ago, I dabbled in a club near my old bar, Ritz Russo's. I was becoming a regular there, watching the girls dance, but never wanting one enough to invite them for drinks after their shift. I took mild interest in some, but never followed through with any. It's better when I watch anyway. I'm not ready to fucking feel again. I thought I'd come here and things would change—that I'd change—but the urges were too strong. The need beckoning me to fulfill the ache won out and here I am…again.

Paying the cover fee, I nod to the bar manager, who scowls at me. For some reason, he's not very taken with me, which is laughable considering the money I spend in his establishment. He can fuck off. I'm not here to see him.

Working part-time as an apprentice at a tattoo parlor while finishing up my art degree just about pays the bills. Luckily for the girl I like to come here to watch—*and me*—I got a nice paycheck when I sold my old man's place so I can continue to fulfill this need.

Making my way to the bar, I drop two hundred dollars down on the smooth surface and slide it toward the bartender, James. "Room twelve available?"

He looks over at the owner, who glares for a few seconds before shaking his head no. What the fuck?

I place another hundred down and quirk a brow. She's worth it. Watching her makes all the other shit in my life fade to nothing. All I see is her in those moments. All I feel is her, even though I can't touch her. The extra hundred is definitely worth it.

Offering me a cocky smile, James takes the key from the hook behind the bar and hands it over to me. Money talks. "Thirty minutes. Enjoy."

Oh, I plan to.

I make my way through the club toward the private viewing rooms in the back. The atmosphere is alive, the sexual tension potent in the air you breathe. Everything is designed to bring your desires to the surface and get the blood flowing—the music a deep, seductive hum; the lighting low and well placed, giving you a sense of obscurity.

At this place, you're free to be you. The girls look at you like you're the only man in the room. Their movements are meant to entice, provoke—and they do. Money, lots of it, leaves the wallets of every guy in here, disappearing into their G-strings.

A few of the private rooms have the red light above, signaling them occupied, but twelve is green.

That light just turned on. Her shift starts at the same time every night, and I'm always the first person here to see her—to watch her.

The key clicks the door open, and the green light flashes before turning red.

She's mine for half an hour.

The room is decorated in black—black walls, black floor, black couch attached to the back wall so you can bring more than one person in if you wanted to, but not me. This is my time. My elixir.

The glass wall separating me from her becomes transparent as the light behind it turns on, revealing the square box she performs within.

Right in the center, is her—*Room Twelve*.

Black heels make her legs look impossibly long. My eyes drag up the toned, tanned length, my cock growing in my jeans. Her ass is confined inside a pair of silk panties. Not a G-string like the pole dancers. No, she's no typical stripper.

There's a tease of a tattoo creeping down the panty line of her left ass cheek. A flower possibly? Black leather in the form of a corset encases her torso, making her tits bulge from the top. A lace collar wrapped around her neck has pre-cum dampening the tip of my cock. The dark locks of her hair are bundled up in a loose updo with fallen strands framing her face hidden behind a full black mask.

Not seeing her face is part of the fucking thrill. She could be anyone at any time. We could be in the same class, live in the same building. And yet, she'll never know I watch her. She can't see into the room, due to the mirrored glass on the inside top half of the box, and it makes my heart race.

Her body begins to sway as the music plays through the speaker. I track every inch of her, witnessing her movements like a starved prisoner getting food for the first time in forever. I was last here two nights ago, yet I missed her—missed watching her.

She's fluid with the beat, like water ebbing and flowing with every new direction it's taken in. Her hands roam the planes of her body, moving up and over the tit spillage before running them into her hair and pulling on the string keeping it up. It spills around her, blanketing her slender shoulders and falling like melted chocolate down her back. It's long, nearly reaching her ass. She uses it as an accessory—a tool in her seduction. Her body and the music are one as she lets it consume her. Rolling her head over her shoulders, she makes the waterfall of hair dance for her.

My cock strains, begging for relief.

Unbuckling my belt, I unbutton my jeans and pull my cock free. Wrapping my hand around the meaty girth, I give it a firm tug, using my thumb to rub in the liquid beading over the tip. My jacob's ladder piercing only adds to the pleasure. I imagine the way it would rub along all the tender parts inside her, claiming her with pleasure.

My gaze moves with her, taking in everything.

Nimble fingers pull on the strings of her corset, revealing the flesh of her stomach inch by inch until it loosens over her chest. She pulls it open, revealing big, natural tits with rosy, swollen nipples, hard and in need of sucking. Her corset falls to the floor, and her hands palm her tits, giving them a squeeze. The vein in my cock pulses.

Pulling out my wallet, I pluck out another two hundred dollars and shove it in the little metal drawer at the bottom of the window. Her head snaps to the noise, but she remains still for a few seconds. I pause with her. Waiting, enticing, challenging her.

Why are you hesitating, beautiful?

I let out a relieved sigh when she walks over to the drawer, counts the money, and places it at the back of her box before turning to face the glass and dropping to her knees, parting them. I'm desperate to rip her panties away. Instead, I stand and approach the glass separating us, my cock firmly in my grip.

I watch her trace her hand down her body, disappearing into her silk panties. Her chest heaves as she touches herself. I stroke my cock, fisting it hard in rhythm with her movements, imagining what she sounds like, what those parted lips would feel like around my cock. I want to taste the mist of sweat coating her skin.

Her body begins to tremble as her fingers play with her cunt, the outline of her hand tenting her panties.

My balls draw up in warning. I'm about to come, but I need to see her.

Shoving another hundred into the box, I hold my breath as she appears to stare right into me. I pump at my cock with slow, measured strokes to stop from blowing before I've seen her. She brings her other hand down to drag the material of the panties to the side, and pleasure pulses through me.

Her pretty pink lips, plump and bare, glisten with arousal. She parts them with her fingers, allowing me to see her needy, flushed clit and the juices leaking from the hole I want to stuff my cock in to the fucking hilt.

A warm wave of pleasure buckles my spine. Reaching out to steady myself, I place my hand on the glass as ribbons of cum spurt out of me and decorate the window.

Fuck.

I'm obsessed.

2

Breezy

It's late. I'm tired as hell. And I miss my man.

Which are all the makings for a storm called John. It doesn't matter if I rush to try to get out of here as quick as I can or stall, hoping to slip past him when it's quiet, he'll be waiting for me.

Tonight, I don't have the energy for it.

I sit down on the bench in the dressing room, ignoring the buzz of the other women around me as I rifle through my purse. I'm trying to sort my head out. Disgust ripples through me, making me shudder.

This place has officially ruined me.

Sucked me into the pit of its belly and spit me

out. I'm filth shoved back into the world. Ruined and dirty. No longer the fresh-faced, happy girl I once was. This place has turned me into a piece of shit.

The only thing that keeps me from going down the toilet of despair is Christian.

Handsome. Brilliant blue eyes. A killer smile.

I don't deserve him, yet I defied the laws of the universe and have him anyway.

Knock. Knock. Knock.

Clarissa, a busty blonde who does a lot of Dolly Pardon looks, prances over to the door to answer it. I cringe knowing my time for hiding is over.

"Hey, Johnny baby," Clarissa coos, her voice dripping with fakeness. Every girl in here can't stand John. But John signs our paychecks so we have to pretend. "Sure thing, doll. She's changing, but I'll send her out."

She closes the door and rolls her eyes at me before prancing back over to her table. While some of the girls are kind of snobby at times, they usually weed themselves out after a few weeks. The long haulers—Clarissa, Ginny, Becks, Leslie, and myself—look out for each other.

I let out a heavy sigh. He'll wait outside that

door forever. And frankly, I don't have forever. I'm tired, and if I want to go to the movies with Christian tomorrow, I need to be rested.

Sucking in a deep breath, I attempt to calm my jitters. I'm feeling extra rattled. Of all the years I've worked here, tonight nearly broke me.

I was turned on.

Another wave of disgust washes over me. I can't wait to get home, stand under the hot spray of the shower, and scrub away the filth seeping through my pores.

I should quit.

Tears burn my eyes. As delightful as that seems, it doesn't feel like a reality to me. I need these hours, and I stupidly got hooked on the money—money I need. One day, I'll save enough to change the course of my life, but for now, I'm stuck.

I just can't let the customers get to me. Normally, I don't. But this guy—Mr. Benjamins is what I call him since he makes it freaking rain hundred dollar bills—finally got to me.

Why is he so obsessed with me?

Each time he watches me—which is becoming frequent—he gets more and more demanding with what he wants from me. Simply waves his money and tosses it into the tray. And like an addict, I greedily snatch it up and give him what he wants. His urgency and need to see all of me worked its way inside me. It's been that way for weeks now. Each time, he gets bolder and more desperate. Apparently, I'm right there with him, because I'm not leaving the job anymore. It follows me home, finds its way into my shower, haunts my dreams.

Last night, I came with mental images of what Mr. Benjamins looks like. The window in the hot box allows me to see his bottom half, but it's mirrored at the top half, preventing me from getting a good look. All I ever see is his thick, veiny cock lined with his scarily hot piercings. I'd moaned in the shower like I was putting on a show for him. When the orgasm subsided, I was left feeling hollow and used. And I did it to myself.

Tonight, he wanted to see all of me.

And I nearly gave in, barely keeping the scrap of panties on. Losing the panties is a huge no-no at the club.

I fell right back into the fantasy of it like I had in the shower. Knowing he was stroking himself in tandem with the way I touched myself made me slick with need. He saw just how aroused I was for him. The evidence was all over my fingers. I squirm on the bench seat. My panties are wet again.

Sick, Breezy. You're sick.

I swallow down the bile from my self-hatred and rise on unsteady legs. Forcing a smile on my face, I grab my bag and wave to the girls getting ready to leave for the night. The moment I open the door, I find John Wendell leaning against the velvet covered wall. As soon as he sees me, his green eyes light up.

"Hey, Summer," John greets, a wide grin stretching across his face.

"Hey, hunk."

He beams, loving how I still flirt with him. It's my fault really. When he hired me, I'd been so desperate for a job, I said things I knew would get me a place here at The Hot Box. At first, the playful banter had been refreshing. I heard horror stories about exotic dance clubs, so I had been expecting the worst. John was a thirty-year old handsome man who was always smiling and seemed like a good guy to work for. Once the newness faded, I realized he's like every other strip club owner: greasy, demanding, dirty, ruthless. John's never put his hands on me like he has with some of the other girls when he loses his temper, but that's because he wants me.

With me, he tries extra hard to show me what a gentleman he is. To show me how generous and kind he is. And while it's worked in my favor with pay and hours, it's destroyed my happiness. He's a clingy film stuck to my skin, and no matter how hard I scrub, he's staining me.

"Want to grab a coffee?" he asks, stepping forward and assaulting me with his cloying cologne.

"You're so sweet," I coo, "but you know I need to get back home. It's late."

His hand finds my hip over my yoga pants and he caresses me. "You could come home with me, Summer."

A forced giggle escapes me. "Can't, baby. I'm a one-man girl. You know that."

"I can share," he teases back.

That, I don't believe.

John is obsessed about shit. And right now, he's obsessed with me. Sharing isn't in his vocabulary. It's just more crap he spews in hopes I'll cave and fall into his bed.

"You're a mess," I say with a smile that hurts as I try to step away.

He walks forward, tightening his grip on my hip. "We both know you're good for me. Just let it happen." His palm finds my ass, giving it a squeeze. "Just let it happen."

Gently, I press my hand to his chest and push him back.

His face pinches in displeasure. "Summer." My *name*—the name I've demanded he and everyone else here call me despite what's on my driver's license—on his lips feels like a warning. Like he's played my game and wants to change the rules.

"See you soon, baby," I purr, batting my lashes at him and grinning.

I turn and try not to run down the hall away from him. I barely make it to the door at the end of the hallway when an arm sweeps around my waist, pulling me back. John caresses my ribs as he nuzzles my hair. I freeze and close my eyes, hoping he'll just let me go.

"I was thinking about putting you on the floor," he murmurs, his hot breath tickling my ear.

I swallow down the lump in my throat. The floor is for brave girls like Clarissa or Leslie. The floor is for the girls who can shake their assets in front of a crowd and earn a shit ton. The boxes are for girls like me—the ones who detest who they've become—a place to hide away their shame. We earn our money privately.

"You know I'd be horrible out there," I say lightly, trying to hide the tremble in my tone. "Besides, I only really have one customer these days. I'm bad for business." My teasing words don't cut through the tension.

"The boxes are for my favorites," John rumbles, his palm sliding dangerously close to my pussy over my pants. "I've kept you locked away in that box for a long time, Summer. Saving you for myself. But…" His unspoken words hang in the air.

But if you don't want me, I'll give you to them.

Turning in his arms, I tilt my head up and flash him a fake smile. "I'm still your favorite," I flirt. I press my lips to the corner of his mouth. "Don't forget that."

His eyes darken as his palms grip my ass in a possessive way. "It'd be easier to remember if you'd let me spend more time with you."

"We'll grab coffee soon, baby," I lie. "When I'm not so tired. I have a big day with Christian tomorrow."

He flinches at the reminder, but remains undeterred. "I'll win you over one day."

"Of course you will," I say with a bright smile before tugging from his grip. "See you tomorrow, John."

Sometimes I wish I could call in sick.

As soon as I climb into my Honda, I rest my forehead on the steering wheel and choke out a sob. Why is this my life? In the privacy of my own space, I cry like the weak woman I've become. For so long, I've been strong and fierce. I've trucked along despite the shitty hand life has dealt me. I've made lemonade from lemons.

But I'm tired.

Something has to give.

When all my tears are wrung out, I swipe at my wet cheeks with the heels of my hands and start my car. I'll go home, shower off the grime The Hot Box leaves on me, and try to enjoy tomorrow with my man.

I sit up straight and tap into my reserve of inner strength that seems to darken each day. At one time, it flared brightly and fearlessly. One day, I hope I'll find a way to stoke that fire again.

Until then, I'll go home and sleep off my bad night.

Tomorrow, I'll start again.

3

Lucca

We're strangers of the night, yet I feel more connected to her than anyone else. Both of us broken in some way, banished to the dark world of depravity, creeping around unseen by the rest of world. You have to be damaged to do a job like this—to let men watch you dance naked for their pleasure. *Does she need saving?*

I'm on alert for no reason. She doesn't even work Mondays, yet the chance we could be in the same room and not even know it sends a rush of adrenaline through my veins.

There's a relaxed pulse of music humming from the speakers and a few women dancing on poles while the rest work the crowd.

Flesh is on display everywhere you look, and I can't help my eyes from going to every ass on show, checking for her tattoo. It's fucking ridiculous. Even if she did work tonight, she's never out here in the main bar with the lap dancers.

I shouldn't be propped up at the bar like a fucking loser looking for one glimpse of the little bunny who's caught the hunter's eye, but I can't help myself. The impulse is too strong. So here I am. Out front in the main bar pretending to be entertained by the overly nice girls showing all their skin in the hopes a wealthy pervert will deposit his week's wage into their G-string. And this place is full of those types: middle aged men in suits wearing their wedding rings without any fucking shame. The truth is, I envy those bastards. I wish all I needed was a lap dance every now and then from whoever was willing. Instead of having this ache and compulsion to watch—*to see her*. These other girls don't do anything for me. Just her. Internally, I curse myself for even coming in here tonight. I don't like being in the main bar on show.

Inconspicuous, lurking in the shadows, just watching, is where my buzz comes from—and where I prefer to be. I don't want gyrating, impersonal lap dances from girls with fake tits who like bouncing them under my chin.

My little dancer has a hold on me these other girls can't touch. It's consuming. A darkness calling out to me. I can't ignore it or walk away. It's an addiction. A thirst never quenched. My pulse spikes just thinking about her hidden behind the glass from me. No one since my ex has elicited this sort of response from me.

She'd run from me if she knew just how under my skin she's become.

I want to smell her, watch her in her own environment. See what she looks like when she doesn't think anyone is watching. Would she be as intoxicating? *Yes.*

I order another beer despite knowing I have to be up early for work in the morning. Going back to an empty apartment and looking at the same four damn walls doesn't appeal to me.

A blonde with big tits and ass implants sidles up next to me, stroking her finger down my arm. "You want a dance, handsome? I'm the best there is," she coos.

Smirking, I lick my lips, giving her a once over, pretending to like what I see.

"I'm sure you are, darling. But maybe another time." I pull out some bills and slip them under her bra strap.

"Suit yourself," she says with a shrug, sauntering over to another man who acts almost giddy at the prospect she chose him. *Like it's not just a job to her.*

"Your favorite girl just showed to cover for another girl," the bartender says, winking at me before placing a beer on the bar and nodding behind me.

My dick sparks to life. Was he talking to me? I check beside me to make sure. I'm alone, and the beer is in front of me, so he means *my* dancer is here.

She's here.

I'm reluctant to turn around. Do I want to break the veil we have? Ruin something really fucking good? She's my strange addiction, and I like it. Would it fade away if I saw her without the glass barrier?

Sucking in a breath, my head turns without permission, my eyes seeking her out. My chest tightens when I see the back of a woman wearing jean shorts and a white tee at the rear of the club just inside an open door. Her dark brown hair is loose down her back, and her body is in the arms of the grimy club owner. *It's her.*

Now it makes sense why that prick doesn't like me. "They an item?" I query the bartender with a wicked smirk, knowing the owner no doubt has bitched about me to him.

Shaking his head, he slings a towel over his shoulder and places his hands on the bar, leaning into me. "He wants to be. Summer? Not so much."

Summer.

Heat burns through me like the rays of the sun.

Knowing her name makes me feel like even more of a stalker.

Her posture is rigid. She doesn't like being touched by him. He's a cunt who thinks because the girls work in a place like this, it's an open invitation for him to be able to grope and fuck them whenever he wants. The more upscale places detest club owners like him.

I crane my neck to get a better view, and it's as if the room falls silent and my vision tunnels.

I grip the beer bottle in my hand, clenching my fist to stop myself from doing something crazy like waltzing back there, stealing her out of his grasp, drop kicking the slimy fuck, and whisking her away for my own pleasure.

She pulls away from the dick and shakes her head no at something he asks. I'm transfixed, yet want to look away all at the same time. This makes her real—a person, not the fantasy I have in my head of who she is.

I feel nervous for some fucked up reason, like this will impact my life, become a pivotal moment.

Just as she turns to face me, I tense all over in anticipation, then the door closes, hiding her from view. *Fuck.*

Inhaling a lungful of air, not even realizing I'd been holding my breath, I laugh and shake my head. This isn't fucking healthy.

Her name is Summer.

Summer.

Summer.

Summer.

Fuck, I am a stalker.

"You want to reserve her room?" the bartender asks, grinning.

I down the rest of my beer and push the bottle toward him. "Nah, I'm good," I lie, like a pathetic loner. Damn, I need to get myself some company.

With a slap of a twenty on the counter, I make my way through the crowded club to find the blonde from earlier.

Pulling out a wad of cash, I crook my finger

at her. She grins like a cat that got the cream and abandons the guy she was working to follow me to a booth at the back of the club.

As soon as my ass hits the leather, she straddles my lap. She smells of vanilla and a mix of men's cologne. God knows how many laps she's been on tonight alone.

Her blonde hair whispers over my face as she pushes her tits into my chest and thrashes her head. Each beat of the music causes her to twist and move, her big ass grinding down on my dick. She's not unattractive, just too…"in my face" and not my type.

An announcement comes through the room about the private rooms being open and the list of girls dancing tonight. When they say Summer, I will myself to resist paying for her room.

I'm not a stalker.

I can walk away.

Pushing the blonde from my lap, I stuff some bills in her G-string and slap her ass.

"We can have more time, baby. Tell me what you like," she purrs, running her hands down her tits and squeezing.

"Not you," I grunt before walking away.

Fifteen minutes, that's how long it takes to walk

home, and every inch of the way will be spent resisting the urge to turn around and go back.

But I'm stronger than that.

I'm not a stalker.

I walked away.

•••••▬•••••

I fall through the door of the tattoo shop twenty minutes late. Couldn't sleep last night pacing my apartment with nothing to do but think. It's a slow torture. Insomnia's a bitch.

"You're late," my boss and friend Jake states with a quirk of his pierced brow.

Jake is an oddity. He has all the brute and style of a biker, but the face and manners of a pretty choirboy. Women come in here to get tats just as an excuse to drop their pants for him. He's fucking good at his craft, though, and I struck gold getting an apprenticeship with him.

I don't think about the favor my baby sister's boyfriend pulled to get me in here. Ronan Hayes isn't a man I want to owe anything to, but I'm also not as stubborn as I used to be and can see an opportunity when it's presented to me.

I spent years of my life raising my sister after our dad died. Gave up school and lost the woman I thought I'd spend my life with—all for my sister, Sofina. Unfortunately, I was angry and bitter for most of those years. Clipped her wings without even realizing I was dulling her colors.

Ronan is a prick, but he loves her and has been real fucking good to her. I'm learning to take the losses. Everyone leaves in the end. It's why I don't fucking trust people anymore. Why I like to watch from a distance.

"You still asleep?" Jake snorts when I haven't said anything.

"Sorry, man. Crashed late. Slept through my alarm."

"You should see a doctor. Get some pills. I've got some ganja if you want some to help you sleep."

"Yeah, I might take you up on that. For now, I'll survive on these." I smirk, holding up an energy drink.

The buzz in this place is relaxed and has more of a family vibe than coworkers. Jake built his reputation, and this shop, from the ground up with his own sweat and tears. It's a well-established place.

Appointments are booked months in advance. And every year, Jake and his team travel for conventions and competitions. I hope to be going with them this year.

Dumping my things in the back room, I come through the shop to see both the other artists already busy with clients. They offer a head nod, which I mimic.

"You want to sit in and watch my eleven o'clock? It's a continuation of an original design she brought in. Pretty sick." Jake rubs his hands together in excitement.

"Yeah, sounds good. Where's she having it done?" I move over to his station and look around to see if anything needs to be wiped down.

"Started on her ass cheek and will be moving down the upper thigh." He nods to the images he has pinned up. I scan over them, and my insides twist. That's real fucking familiar—and not just because I recognize the edges of the flowers, but because the drawing is an original all right.

An original of my fucking design.

4

Breezy

A breeze lifts my dress as I walk up to the tattoo parlor for my meeting with Jake. I quickly push it down, hoping I'm not giving the entire street a show. Funny how that's exactly what I do for a living, but the moment I'm outside the club doors, I morph back into me. No free shows for anyone.

I'm early, so I stop to grab a soda from the shop next door. I should be nervous, the meatier parts of the flesh hurt more, but it's kind of an addictive pain. *God, I'm going to hell.*

I found Jake's place a couple years ago. I'd been in a bad place emotionally. Helpless. Alone. Sad as hell. It took a lot of courage to make an appointment and start on a piece that will eventually go up most of my back and nearly to the back of my knee along my thigh. When I first brought the picture to Jake, I wasn't sure what he could do with it. It was small—meant to go on the bicep or one shoulder blade. A challenge. And back then, I could never resist a challenge.

Now?

Between the club and the turn my life took years ago, I'm not just broken, I'm completely snapped in half. My will, my drive, my desires were all stuffed into a box and chained shut. It's like a crashing wave has doused my inner fire that moved me to do everything.

Taking that small challenge, designed in ink, was my first attempt to get a hold on the life that had been crumbling before me. After Jake got past his hard-on over the design, he was game to ink it on me. When I told him I wanted it bigger and for him to expand on it, he actually laughed at me. I wanted to start on my ass as a little "fuck you," then grow it into something epic and beautiful. He took that challenge and ran with it. Everything else in my life may be based on what I have to do to make ends meet, but this tattoo is one of the only things I have left reflecting the old me.

Jake's shop is known for their artistic flair. They're not like most shops which copy designs. Jake and his crew are the real deal. Even with my design. Once he realized I was serious about making it huge, he had to sit with it for a while and come up with a design that complemented what was already drawn, then fit it to my body. Now, it's a matter of time and money—there never seems to be enough of either—as I slowly add to it little by little.

After paying for my soda, I make my way next door. A prickle of awareness heats my skin as I walk past the shop window. The same feeling I get when I'm in the box. Rather than feeling owned by it, I seek out the source. Several men on motorcycles parked outside the shop look me up and down, no shame in being caught checking me out. Most women would probably bask in their attention—pleased to have snagged their eye. For me, I hate it. The club has conditioned me to hate it. It makes me rethink the sunny yellow dress I wore knowing Jake would need easy access. It makes me wish I had worn flip flops—despite the chilly air—rather than high wedges that make my legs look shapelier. And it certainly makes me wish I weren't wearing a simple thong beneath the thin fabric.

Mimicking their stares, I push the door open with my back, keeping my eyes on them, letting them know I see them watching. A warmth trickles over me, once again reminding me of the person I've become—the person who's sometimes aroused when they watch. The bell jangles as I back into the shop. I'm hit with a sterile scent and subtle smoky smell that reminds me of the club.

A throat clears.

Something about the impatience of it is a hard clench to my heart. I abandon looking at the bikers through the glass door and turn. The hairs on my arms stand on end. A small shudder trembles through me. And the soda in my hand drops, crashing to the ground and fizzing everywhere.

All eyes shoot up to look at me. I feel fucking faint. Am I dreaming?

"It *is* you!"

That voice.

A thousand memories. A thousand kisses. A thousand promises.

I'm assaulted by a past I try desperately to

forget each day.

No.

Dropping down to pick up the can, I gulp down a lungful of air. I hope I'm imagining this. Not a chance. I stand and lock eyes with the familiar, probing and intense blue eyes of none other than Lucca Russo. His eyes—oh my God they stab at my heart—lock with mine, anger flaring in them.

Anger?

Hell no.

He has not one single thing to be angry about.

But me? I'm fuming.

"Be with you in a second," Jake calls from his station. "Your timeliness will be the death of me." I don't reply, my focus trained on one thing.

Lucca marches toward me, a furious wave rippling from him.

Thud. Thud.

"Lucca? What the fuck?" Jake frowns, but Lucca only has eyes and words for me.

Before he can speak, I do.

Fuck him and his glare.

"What are you doing here?" I demand, the snuffed out fire inside my chest blazing into an inferno only Lucca had been able to manage.

His devastatingly handsome face twists into a cruel sneer—a sneer he'd saved for lots of people in the past, but never me. Not until the end. Not until now.

"Me?" His laugh is cold and mocking, his familiar scent engulfing me as he comes to rest a mere foot from me. "I work here. What are *you* doing here?"

I swallow down the emotion clawing its way up inside me. "I have an appointment." I cross my arms over my chest. His blue eyes dart there briefly, making my skin heat, before he mimics the action. With him standing there, his biceps bulging and dark hair in disarray, I'm reminded of so many times together with him. Pain slices through me, nearly debilitating.

He left me.

He stole everything he ever created within my heart and took it when he bailed on me.

My eyes burn with tears. I fist my hands, wishing I could hit him for every time he made me cry from his absence. My lip wobbles, and I bite down on it. Of course, Lucca's stare drops there. He never misses a detail. Cold indifference contorts his face into a deadly expression—a hateful one I've only ever seen once.

"That's my design," he says stubbornly.

Anger surges back inside me like the swell of a wave, building with desperation to decimate before crashing down. "It was a gift," I hiss, my upper lip curling. *"Mine."*

He scoffs, and his cruel expression hardens. *"You were mine."*

I blink at him in shock. "And *you* left me."

Our voices have risen, and several people become interested in our argument. I'm only interested in slapping the shit out of him. After feeling dead for so long, the anger swirling inside me feels good. I certainly feel alive. Someone opens the front door, and the wind whips after me, fluttering up my dress again, drawing Lucca's eyes to my thighs.

"Hi. I have an appointment with Layne," a woman says, standing next to me awkwardly, sensing she's walked in on a moment.

"Back here, Rena!" Layne calls out.

Jake appears with a giant roll of paper towels.

"Take it outside, Russo," he grinds out. "Make it quick."

I can hear the irritation in Jake's voice. Of course he doesn't want his employee and customer to have a nuclear meltdown in the front of his shop. Bad for business.

Lucca grips my bicep in a possessive way that used to have me swooning. Now, it makes me jolt from his sudden touch. Still warm. Still firm. I try to jerk from his hold, but he simply growls in frustration before hauling me out the door. He guides me around the side of the building and away from prying ears. As soon as we're in the alleyway, he glowers at me, his gaze raking over me from head to toe.

"I can't believe you even have the audacity to twist that shit around on me," he snarls, the muscles in his neck making his tattoo seem to breathe with life.

"Twist it on you? Lucca, you left me!" This time, the tears build, and one lets loose. I hastily swipe it away, harnessing my anger.

He steps closer, and my ass hits the brick wall. I hate how my body responds to him, even after all this time. He sets me on fire in a way no one else ever could. The control he has after all this time is infuriating. It's my fault. I never let him go, and now that he's back, the pull is strong, and I can't help but go with it.

"I left because I had to," he utters lowly, a brief flash of pain in his blue eyes. "Sofina was just a teenager. She had no one, Autumn."

My real name on his lips sends a deep, familiar tingle down my spine. And I hate it. I hate that he's inside me and doesn't have to do a thing to earn that.

"I had no one," I cry out, shoving his hard chest. The bastard doesn't move, simply closes in on me. "I had no one."

His features soften slightly as he studies my face up close. He frowns when his gaze skims over my wet cheek. I freeze as his hand rises. With the gentlest of touches, he swipes away the tear stain with his rough thumb. Then, as though he's breaking from a spell, he glares at me.

"You never listened that day," he hisses, not moving away from me. His heat blankets my flesh. "You ranted about what you wanted and didn't give a shit that I wanted the same thing."

A sob chokes me, but I swallow it down. "Of course I gave a shit!" Another tear races out. He swipes this one away too. "You were so upset about your father and your new obligation to your sister, but you never gave us a chance to work it out. You didn't even want to try. Just got pissed off and sent me away." I want nothing more than to grab the front of his T-shirt and fall against his massive, warm chest. Instead, I affix my bitchiest glare. These tears are angry, not sad. *Lies.*

The wind howls past us, sending my dress blowing up between us. A possessive growl rumbles from him as he slides his large hands down my body and pushes the material back down to cover me.

Bitter tears leak out.

If only he knew everyone in this damn town with a working dick has seen what's under this dress. Shame coats over my skin. Disgust ripples through me. I did what I had to do—something I would have never done had he stayed.

The wind blows again, but he presses his hips against me, pinning the material between us. My dark hair plasters to my face. In a surprisingly gentle and familiar way, he uses one finger to pull the hair from my eyes and tuck it behind my ear.

I can't take this.

I can barely take seeing him and talking to him and smelling him, much less touching him.

"I had to leave," he tells me, his voice the softest since we first spoke a few minutes ago inside. "I had to."

"You didn't," I breathe out, resentment leaking into my words, making me sound like a bitch. "You could have stayed."

His body goes rigid. "My sister needed me."

I needed you.

I slide my palm to his chest with every intention of pushing him away, but can't help but linger over his heart where the beat thrums hard beneath my fingertips, right under where my nickname is inked. *Breezy.*

"I need to go," I state in a cold voice I hope freezes him to his bones. "I have my appointment, and I need to be somewhere after this. I can't run late."

"We're not done talking about this, Autumn," he growls, his blue eyes hardening once more.

But we are.

Autumn isn't who I am anymore.

He shut me down six years ago.

It's too little too late.

I was forced to move on without him, whether I liked it or not. My life moved like currents in the ocean, dragging me far away from him. Each day was a struggle not to drown. I've barely stayed afloat.

And now he's back.

Glaring at me like the sun itself. It's so hard not to reach for him—to get burned by him. But six years ago, he hurt me in a way I'll never recover from. I can't emotionally afford for it to happen again.

"Goodbye, Lucca," I utter in my most hateful tone, pushing on his chest. This time, he steps away, a dark expression marring his features.

"You can't just walk away," he bites out. "We're not done."

You walked away from me. We've been done ever since.

"You can't just walk away," he says, firmer. Like if he says it harshly enough, I'll obey. His voice softens to nearly a whisper. "Autumn, you can't just walk away." A plea this time—one that threatens to tear what's left of my broken heart into shreds.

But I *can* leave him.

I can be cruel too.

I learned from the best.

"Watch me."

5

Lucca

A cruel joke. That's what I thought as soon as I saw Autumn—or fucking Summer—whatever the fuck she goes by these days—walk through the shop door two days ago.

My dancer girl was my ex-girlfriend.

The one who tore my heart out when she refused to come with me after my dad died.

My two worlds colliding knocked the wind out of me, and I've been moping around my apartment, trying to forget about them both, still struggling to combine the two entities as being the same damn person.

That tattoo! How had I not recognized it? It was

my design staring at me from the cheek of her ass every damn time she danced for me. It wasn't until the full print on Jake's wall glared back at me like some fucked up hidden camera show that it came flooding back. I designed it for her after she asked me to deflower her on our fifth date.

Shit, she was cute, and I couldn't wait to pop that damn cherry.

How had I not known it was her? I'd studied that entire body from head to toe. Tasted and fucked her in every position. *She's changed.*

Those legs were one of the first things I noticed about Autumn. She was the university tour guide. Her mother worked in reception, so Autumn knew that place inside and out.

She wore a yellow sundress that kept lifting in the breeze, making her freak out and trying to contain it. I felt like a horny teenager right then and there for the girl in the sundress. Three months later, we were joined at the hip. I nicknamed her Breezy. She was conservative and sweet, and I was a rogue asshole to anyone but her. We were opposites, but we had a fire that kept burning, gaining heat—until my dad died and I had to move away.

WATCH *Me*

Six Years Ago…

The slamming of the front door, followed by light footfalls, lets me know Autumn's arrived after I sent her an urgent text message asking her to meet me at my shitty apartment.

"This better not be a booty call, Luc. I skipped a lecture," *she singsongs, coming into the room and throwing her bag onto a nearby chair.*

So casual. So domestic. So normal.

My solemn face alerts her to the severity of me wanting to see her. Her arms fold under her tits, and she begins chewing her fat, juicy bottom lip. She's so breathtaking, I want to sink into her heat and forget the call I got earlier. Her short brown hair bounces around her shoulders as she shifts from foot to foot.

"What is it, Luc?" *She sounds hoarse, a lump already building in her throat.*

Pain radiates through me. All consuming. Devastating. Debilitating. Not only am I aching from loss, but I'm struggling under the new burden I bear. The thought of going at it alone scares the fucking shit out of me.

"My dad died," I blurt out, gazing up at her from the couch.

Fuck. Saying it out loud makes it that much more real.

Her expressive eyes widen, then she's on her knees in front of me, dragging my hands into hers. I live in a cheap ass apartment I rent with two other students, but this had become home. My life. It's all about to go away.

"I'm sorry, babe. What can I do?" she coos, sadness glimmering in her eyes.

Be with me. Just fucking be with me.

"You can say yes when I ask you to move back with me," I tell her honestly, my voice gruff with emotion. I don't know how my life is about to change, but I want her to change with it. I need for her to change with it.

A weird, strangled laugh comes from her, and she drops my hands. "Move back where with you? Are you joking right now, Lucca?"

A chill settles in my bones at her shrill tone.

"I have to go home, Breezy. Sofina needs me. Dad fucking died." I choke on my words, sucking in a calming breath. "She's going to be put into the foster system unless I do something about it." And that's not

fucking happening. "Dad's bar needs to be managed. Fuck." *There's so much to do. So much that now weighs heavily on my shoulders. All I want to do is crawl into bed with my girl and fuck away the stress.* "I'm leaving. I have to."

She rises to her feet, a panicked expression marring her pretty face. "Y-You're leaving me?"

Standing with her, I reach out, grasping her face between the palms of my hands. "No, I'm asking you to come home with me."

"But t-this is our home, Luc." *She frowns, waving around the shitty apartment as tears streak down her cheeks.*

I knew she'd respond this way, yet I put myself out there anyway. For love. Breezy's life has always been scheduled and orderly. It wasn't until I blew through her world like a damn hurricane that she lived and let go a little. I'm trying to pluck her from the life she's designed to come help me parent my sister and run my dad's bar. It's a longshot, but it's one I'm hellbent on taking.

"No, this shithole was never home." *Releasing her, I shake my head, running my hands through my hair.* "You're home. Sofina is home."

"W-What about school?" *she cries out.* "You only have a year left! Less even!"

Like I can worry about myself or school right now. Life shoved me down, and I'm just trying to get the fuck back up. Nothing is about me. I have a young girl to think about who will need food on the table and a roof over her head.

"This isn't a choice," I bark, anger surging up inside me. Feels a lot fucking better than the hurt. "Sofina fucking needs me. Tell me you get that."

Her bottom lip pouts out. "Why can't she come here?"

Snorting, I wave my hands around the place. "Is that a fucking joke? A shitty apartment with three college guys? She has school, a house, a life."

Tears build in her eyes, and she paces the floor, one hand on her hip while the other rubs at her neck—a clear tell she's going to cry.

"You have a life here, school, me!" she cries out, her bottom lip trembling. "Lucca."

I grab her wrists and push her against the wall, my body closing in tight against hers.

Tears drip to her cheeks as her eyes roam my face. "Don't leave me," she pleads.

"Don't let me," I whisper back before tasting the salty wetness from her lips.

She climbs my body, desperate to get as close as possible. Our lips crash and nip. Messy and fucking *chaotic—just the way I like it. Grabbing her thighs, I help her anchor her body around my waist. My dick grows rock hard from the heat of her pussy as she grinds her hips.*

"*Fuck me, Luc. Please. I need to feel you inside me,*" *she implores, needy and breathless.*

Fumbling with my zipper, I manage to push my jeans down my ass, and I rip at her panties, tearing them in half and leaving them dangling from her body.

I feel fucking crazed. Like this is the beginning and end all in one.

Her hot, wet tongue duels with mine, touching every part of the inside of my mouth like she's mapping the thing to her memory.

My cock grows and prods at her pussy, wanting entry. She's tight, but soaked with need. Thrusting my hips up, I ram into her heat, sighing into her mouth at the intrusion. Juices coat my cock, every ridge and vein stroking her insides as I take deep pulls in and out of her body.

Fisting a handful of her hair, I pin her to the wall and take everything from her. Teeth draw blood, and we bite and taste.

"*Come home with me, Breezy,*" *I demand.*

Thrust. Thrust. Thrust.

"*I can't. I have school,*" *she pants, her eyes wild and red cheeks stained with tears.*

Pulling out of her, I drop her thigh and move away so she has to catch herself. Her arousal glistens on my dick and her own thighs. It's picture worthy. I want to keep it on me so I can revisit her scent. She wobbles, but catches her balance. Her hair is in disarray, and there's a wild look in her eyes, like an animal in heat or about to attack. Feral and eager.

Reaching for the lapels of her button-up dress, I tug hard, until all the buttons ping off and clatter on the hard floor. Heavy, full tits bounce, her nipples tightening with the breeze kissing over her bare flesh. I fucking love that she refuses to wear a bra. Material that once resembled her panties hangs in shreds around her waist.

"You can run Dad's bar with me," I say, hating the thought of having to do that myself. "We can do it together. All this will be okay as long as we do it together."

A fresh tear leaks from her eye as she gently shakes her head. "I can't be a glorified bartender, Lucca. I've worked too hard for my degree. Don't ask me to give all that up."

I'm a selfish bastard, but I can't bear the thought of her not coming with me. "Do you love me?"

"That's not fair," she chokes, slipping the dress down her arms, followed by the destroyed panties. She's standing there in nothing but a ratty pair of Converse, and *she's never looked more beautiful—sorrow shining from her tear-stained eyes.*

Life's not fucking fair. I'm learning that.

Her words aren't the ones I want to hear. Breezy and I sometimes communicate better without them. I'll make her see. I'll make her understand. I'll convince her.

I move to the couch and throw my ass down, taking my cock and stroking up the length, squeezing the mushroomed head. She knows what I want before I even open my mouth.

"Show me how much you ache for me. Touch your pussy, Breezy."

She's already walking to the couch, stopping at the small coffee table a foot from me. Lifting her leg, she rests it on the glass surface and bites her lip. Her fingers grope at her hard nipples, tweaking and twisting them before moving down her body. Goosebumps rise over her skin, and I'm thankful my roommates keep this place cold. Cheap bastards.

"I love you," she whispers as her fingertips dip past her navel to between her thighs, spreading her pussy lips for me—glistening pink perfection.

Come back home with me.

"I love you too," I rumble. "Now, fuck your tight hole like you're alone, baby." I pray to fuck that won't be a

reality soon. I can't not have her in my life. She's everything to me.

Tipping her head back, she groans out my name, caressing her clit while dipping two fingers inside her cunt with the other hand.

My cock strains and pulses, pre-cum beading from the tip.

She plows her fingers in and out of her pussy, the intensity picking up steam. She looks fucking crazy sexy. Her tits bounce with her movements. Her stomach tightens and curls over as her orgasm hits fast and hard.

I'm fisting my cock, rubbing in firm tugs, until I'm about to explode. I hold off, keeping myself on edge. Blood rushes through my body, making me insane with want.

Lying back on the couch, I say, "Come sit on my face, Breezy."

Panting heavily, she trembles, walking over to me and straddling my face.

I could recognize her scent anywhere, unique and delicious. Mine. She tastes of the ocean breeze on freshly showered skin. I grip her thighs, pinning her pussy to my face, licking at her release from moments before. Moans muffled from her legs tease my ears, and I groan in response—devouring her—eating out her pussy like it's the last time I'll ever have her on my tongue. Her body jerks and writhes on me, hypersensitive and still desperate for cock.

Lapping her up, I flick my tongue over her clit, bringing her to the edge, then force her backward until she's on her back on the couch between my legs.

"Come home with me," I growl, my tone fierce and commanding. "Autumn, please."

Her brows scrunch together. "I can't, Lucca."

The ache in my chest is beginning to hurt so bad, I can't think straight. My responsibilities, the death of my father, the slipping away of my girl. I can't take this shit.

Getting up on my knees, I stroke my cock hard and fast, looking down over her splayed out for me. She fondles her tits and lifts her hips in offering for me to take her pussy. But I don't. Not yet.

The front door opens and closes, and she stills for a second, her eyes springing open.

"Don't move," I tell her, shifting my hand to her pussy and strumming my thumb over her clit like it's an instrument.

One of my roommates, Gerald, a computer geek, freezes in the doorway, a Twizzler hanging from his open mouth.

I make eye contact with him to let him know I've seen him, but don't stop stroking us both. Dropping my eyes back to Autumn's, I hold her gaze when I push into her heat, plunging hard and deep, making her take all of me.

She'll come with me. I'll remind her how good we're together.

I punish her with brutal thrusts, skin slapping skin, sweat coating our bodies, and she meets me, propelling her hips up to take all my anger, my pain. She lets me bring us both over the threshold of bliss. My dick pulses as my release pumps into her before I pull out and let the ribbons of cum spurt from my cock all over her pussy and stomach, decorating her in my essence. When I've wrung the last drop from my cock, I realize Gerald is gone. Soon, I will be too. I feel fucking sick.

"Don't leave me," Autumn pleads, reading my mind. She reaches out, grasping my forearm, her nails digging in so hard, I'll be left with a mark.

I simply stare at the girl I love. It's like she doesn't get this isn't a choice for me. My choice was to come here for school. I worked hard to make that happen. But life has a funny way of brutalizing its victims. Life has made me its bitch. I don't have a choice, but she does.

I want her to choose me.

"Don't go," she begs.

Fuck, I thought this would be a lot easier. Nothing with Breezy is easy. Nothing worth having ever is.

"Don't make me choose between you and my sister," I grind out, anger chasing away the hurt. "You won't ever win that battle." My words are cold and furious.

She shouldn't put me in that spot to begin with. Choosing.

Her plump lips part, the bottom one wobbling wildly. "D-Do you l-love me?"

Too fucking much.

"Not enough it would appear," I scoff, burning us both with my lie. I rise to my feet and tuck my cock away.

"Lucca…" she breathes, devastation crumpling her features.

I wear my pain slashed all over my bleeding goddamn heart.

"Just go. This is over," I bark, picking up her dress and throwing it at her. "We're over." I'm unreasonable and harsh, but I can't stop myself. There's a rage inside me building, and I can't control it. I'm not enough for her, and I'm going to lose her. My fucking dad's dead, and my sister needs me.

"We can d-do long d-distance," she whimpers, swallowing her pain. "Please. I can't lose you. Don't leave me."

I want to shake her and wake her the fuck up.

"If I want a fuck every other month, I can find someone much closer. Just go. I don't even know why I asked *you to come with me,"* I spit, venomous and cruel. *The walls build up faster than I can stop them. I can't look at the pain in her eyes. It reflects my own.*

"Don't," she sobs. "Please."

"Get the fuck out of here, Autumn. I have packing to do, and you fucking made your choice, so fuck off." *Each hateful word is meant to hurt her, and she flinches at every single one.*

I'm a dick. I want to get on my knees and beg her to come with me, to make everything all right, but pride is a curse, and I allow my anger to lead the way.

She slings her dress on and wraps it around herself since all the buttons are gone. Running past me, she grabs her bag, and without another word, the door slams behind her. A cloud of morbid dread saturates me. Picking up the coffee table, I launch it across the room. It hits the wall and smashes into a hundred pieces, just like my fucking soul.

Present...

I'm pissed all over again. Not at her, but myself. I was unreasonable and selfish. Dropping that shit on her and trying to get her to make a choice on the spot between me and the life she was used to...the career she wanted. What the hell happened to her? How the fuck did my Autumn end up as Summer taking off her clothes for money?

I couldn't think straight after seeing her a couple of days ago, and sure as hell couldn't sit and watch another man tattoo my design on her ass, so I bailed and came home to pace the fucking floor. I've been doing it ever since. It's time to stop pacing and to get some things straightened out. Grabbing my keys, I slam the front door and make my way to her club.

We need to talk, Breezy, and I won't let you blow me off.

6

Breezy

To say I'm shaken is an understatement. With Lucca, he doesn't just shake the ground I walk on…he decimates it. I'm left clawing to remain standing on my own two feet. I hate him for it. I hate him for everything.

Six years.

For six years, I've slowly pieced together my life. Without him. Because of him.

Tears threaten as I walk into the club, but I quickly blink them away. Fuck Lucca. I have Christian now. I'm happy. I'm so happy.

A bitter laugh escapes me. I can't even convince myself.

When I push into the building, the loud music thumps through the air, vibrating my feet as I walk. I'm late. I should care more considering I need the money, but I can't find it in me to give a shit. It's been several days since I saw Lucca, and I'm still shaking.

Autumn, you can't just walk away.

He actually had the audacity to say those words to me.

"Hey, Summer," Becks greets as I enter the dressing room, her lips sparkling. "John is on a fuckin' rampage looking for you. He thinks you quit."

I toss my bag on the bench and frown. "Because I'm late?"

"Because you're an hour late, hon."

An hour?

How long was I sitting in my car?

Crap!

"Are you going out there?" I squeak out as I yank off my T-shirt and toss it on the bench.

"Someone has to go into the box. Your regular is waiting. I didn't want to go," she complains. "You know how claustrophobic I am, but John's losing his shit out there."

Guilt stings me over and over like a swarm of

angry bees. John may not rough me up because I may be one of the few dancers who's held out on fucking him, but it doesn't mean he doesn't hurt anyone else. Becks has come in with her share of bruises—bruises I knew were formed when John grabbed her.

"I've got this," I assure her, yanking off my bra and the rest of my clothes. "You take the floor. I'm sorry you had to deal with his wrath."

She lets out a heavy breath. "He'll be pissed I went against his orders."

"Just lie and tell him I was already in there before you had a chance."

Quickly, I slide on a silky pair of white panties with a black design and a matching bra. I then stuff my feet into high black heels. There's no time to do much else. I give Becks a quick hug of thanks, then bolt down the hallway. I don't see John, thank goodness.

"Hey, Summer," Paul, my usual box bouncer, greets. "Thought Becks was going in the box tonight."

"Change of plans. Thanks, boo," I flirt, flashing him my prettiest smile that always makes the big guy soften.

His lips quirk up on one side as he opens the door for me. "John ain't happy, beautiful."

I stand on my toes and kiss Paul on the cheek. "Cover for me. Tell him I've been here for a while. I'd lie for you, boo."

"Yeah, yeah," he says, grinning. "Been in there for at least a half hour. That's how long your regular's been sitting waiting on you."

Cringing, I nod. "I owe you."

"You know the key to my heart is food."

I force out a laugh, then slip into the small room behind the box. It's tiny. Just big enough for me to suck in a few calming breaths before sliding the door open. A black, full face mask hangs on a hook, and I quickly pull it on to hide my identity. Tonight, I hit the button for a little bit of fog and change the light colors to red. This place is hell. May as well look the part.

A Berlin Scandal song I recognize comes on the speaker. The angry rasp of Xavi Jacobs's tortured voice speaks straight to my soul, filling me with the fire to do what I need to. It's easy to push away the pain of my thoughts from seeing Lucca. I climb into the box and slide the door closed behind me. My nerves are on fire, but I ignore them to begin a sultry dance. Hopefully, Mr. Benjamins will forget I've wasted his time. The last thing I need for him to do is tattle on me.

Last time, he sure wasn't tattling.

No, what I saw was the way he fisted his pierced cock. I'd Googled it the first time I saw it because I'd never seen such a piercing before. A jacob's ladder. Five bars going through the underside of his shaft. Looked super painful, but I couldn't help but wonder how it would feel inside. The veins in his tattooed hand jumped and throbbed with every stroke. I'd been mesmerized at the way he greedily jerked at himself while watching me touch myself.

Needing to give him a show to make up for my tardiness—and hopefully earn me more money—I squat, biting on my bottom lip. With an erotic move, I grip my knees and slide them apart. I grab one of the handles at the top of the box and slowly rock my hips toward the glass. His booted feet move into view, then the familiar scrape of the drawer opening echoes over the music. He drops a bill into the drawer before disappearing beyond my view once again.

I slide two fingers over my panties, a finger on either side of my pussy over the material, and rub.

The fabric is already wet as my mind travels back to Lucca. It feels like a lifetime ago that we were together. And when I saw him, my body had flared back to life, burning with lust and need.

A knuckle raps on the glass, startling me. He's not fisting himself like usual, just standing there, which worries me I'm not doing a good enough job. Needing to up my game, I decide to do what we're not supposed to do.

I take my panties off.

A thrill shoots through me knowing this would infuriate John. It's my body. My tips. With that burst of confidence, I show Mr. Benjamins just how sorry I am for being late. My bra comes off next, until I'm in nothing but my heels. Turning away from him, I bend over and move my hips in a seductive way, taunting him with my wet pussy that he has full access to. I finger my clit, moaning at the delicious zings of pleasure as I look over my shoulder, hoping to catch a glimpse of his impressive dick. When the drawer opens, I bite back a smile. Glancing over, I'm pleased to see a wad of money. He tips well. I need this regular. Coming in late was stupid. I can't let Lucca fuck up my life anymore.

As soon as I stick my finger inside myself, he

knocks hard on the glass. I jolt, yanking my wet finger out and turn around. He slams something up against the window. It's a hundred dollar bill that's scribbled on.

We need to talk.

Oh, shit.

I should holler for Paul, but what do I say? I taunted my customer to the point that I broke the club rules, stripped out of my panties, and practically begged the stranger to fuck me?

I tremble as I scoop the money out of the drawer. His feet disappear, then light floods into the room. He left? Will he report me?

Panic assaults me, and I scramble out of the back of the box. I grab my panties and turn them inside out, ready to put them on, when the door to the small back room opens. It takes me all of two seconds to realize it's not Paul or John. My eyes skim over the boots, and I freeze. It's him. Mr. Benjamins. A large, warm hand grips my hip from behind. I should be running. Not slowly rising, eager to see what he'll do next.

"I used to think watching you was enough. Not anymore."

Lucca?

No.

No. No. No!

I whirl around and face off with Lucca. Again. His handsome features are twisted into an intense mix of fury and lust. I cry out when his hand finds my throat in a domineering way that has both my pulse and pussy fluttering. He tugs off my mask, revealing my shocked face, and tosses it to the floor. I'm not worried about getting fired now. I have more pressing matters to contend with—like Lucca fucking Russo in the box back room with me and his mouth is descending on mine. I let out a mewl of protest, but it gets snuffed out the moment his full lips press to mine.

This is how Lucca talks.

Not with words, but with touches, kisses, caresses. He speaks every time he fucks. I used to love his language. Now, I don't know if I understand it anymore. His groan of pleasure does something inside me. Twists and pulls and tugs. I find my tongue eagerly lashing with his, hungry for his familiar taste.

He slides a hand between us as he kisses me. Gropes my breast and pinches my nipple. I forgot how good it felt to be touched by him. He slides his hand down between my thighs so he can feel the evidence of my arousal.

"Turns you on being watched," he growls. "I created a monster."

It's true. So many times, he'd fuck me, not caring if his roommates saw. I'd loved the thrill of them seeing what they couldn't have—of those nerds he roomed with watching him as he dominated and owned me. And when we'd go in public, he was always testing my limits. Fingering me at the movies or in restaurants. Always seeing how far he could go.

His fingers rub against my clit, and I whimper. I don't know what I'm doing right now, but it feels too good to stop. I'll gather my senses and send him away when it's over, but right this second, I don't want to. I want him to touch and kiss me. I want him to make me feel good. Truth is, I missed him. God, how I've missed him.

"Wait," I moan. "Where's Paul? You can't be in here."

"Money makes people suddenly want to take their break. And, I *am* here," he says in that arrogant tone that used to make me tremble with need.

Used to?

Hell, it still works.

He fumbles with his belt, and I'm in utter shock. Tell him no. Push him away. He's an asshole who left me! Certainly don't assist in frantically pulling at the button of his jeans. Oh my God, I've lost my mind.

Once his jeans are down, he lifts me up by my ass, spreading me out for him. This feels so familiar. Our bodies never forget the deliciously erotic song and dance we have when together.

"You know what I like," he grunts out, barely thrusting his hips against me.

I let out a sharp gasp when his piercings rub along my clit. With a trembling hand, I reach between us, mesmerized at the way the metal feels on my thumb, and ease him to my pussy. He's unbelievably patient as he watches me guide him into me. Once my body sucks the head of his dick inside, I grip onto his shoulders and rock my hips toward him. The first piercing slides past the tender opening of my pussy, making me moan. I pull slightly out of him, somewhat embarrassed at how my cream coats the tip of his dick.

"You like to watch too." His words are cocky, but they send shivers of need rippling through me. "Again, Breezy. Deeper."

At the mention of my nickname, I rock forward again, hissing each time one of the piercings breaches me. It's the weirdest feeling, but I like it. I like it a lot.

"We don't have time for me to try out new tricks now that I have this piercing," he growls. "When I fuck you doggie style, you're going to lose your fucking mind, because I have a feeling those metal balls are going to feel so fucking good for you on your G-spot, baby. But right now, I need to see your face. Fuck, how I've missed this face."

His lips crash to mine as he loses control. Thunderous thrust after thunderous thrust, he drives into me, making me cry out his name, over and over. He somehow manages to pinch my nipples and grip my throat and slap my ass. His hands are greedy and never stay in one place too long—it's as though he's memorizing my flesh.

"Breezy," he groans when his fingers land on my clit. "Come for me, baby. I'm not going to last long. God I've missed this."

He strums me right into ecstasy without much effort. I'm so wound up and overwhelmed, I greedily accept my long overdue orgasm. This sets him off. He groans in such a guttural way, I feel it down to my marrow, and all I can do is accept him—marvel at the way his cock seems to grow in size as he comes and his piercings press into all my tender inner places. A flood of heat surges inside me, waking me from my stupor.

No!

Ugh!

Fucking idiot!

"Get off me," I snap. "You're literally the most irresponsible man I've ever met!"

He pulls away, frowning at me. "What? I'm clean."

I shove at him until I'm standing on my own two feet. His cum runs out of me and down my thigh, thick and potent. Motherfucker.

"I'm not on the pill, asshole!" I slap at his chest again for good measure.

When he gives me his arrogant, smug half-grin, I want to murder him.

"We're over. Have been for some time," I nearly yell at him.

His features harden. "We'll never be over."

"You have two seconds to get the hell out of here and out of my life," I screech, scrambling to pick up my panties and slide them on.

"Autumn," he says with a frown, tucking his

wet cock back in his jeans and fastening them. "Listen."

"One," I threaten as I slide my panties into place and snag up my bra.

"We need to talk."

"Two…"

"Autumn…"

"You've already done enough damage," I spit out as I throw on my bra. "Please leave before you cost me my job too."

He glowers at me for a long, hard second before storming out of the box back room. I tremble, worrying if anyone saw him enter or leave. I attempt to compose myself and suck in several gulps of air.

Stupid, woman. Stupid. Stupid. Stupid!

I snatch up the money he left, feeling disgusting and cheap for doing it, but not dumb enough to leave it for someone else to take.

Shakily, I creak open the door and peek outside. There's no one in the hallway, which makes me wonder where Paul went. I slip out the room and head back toward the dressing room. I push into the dressing room and let out a shriek to find John sitting by my bag, an angry scowl on my face.

Shit. Oh, shit.

John's gaze slides up and down my body. His jaw clenches as he rises to his feet. Panic shoots through me.

"You've been giving guys free shows?" he asks, stalking toward me.

I shake my head in vehemence. "W-What? No!"

"You let them touch you?"

"Never." Not a lie. There is no them. Just him. Just Lucca.

"You let them fuck you?"

"John, no—"

Stars glitter across my vision, and it takes a second to realize he backhanded me. He grabs my throat hard and slams me up against the dressing room door. My head bangs against the wood, dizzying me further.

Tears streak down my cheeks, ruining my makeup. I don't care. All I want to do is get out of here. The money flutters from my hand when John squeezes my throat and I claw at his wrist.

"You think it's okay to lie straight to my face? Like I don't have cameras every-fucking-where?" he snarls, the whiskey on his breath nauseating.

"John, please," I wheeze out.

His hand comes between my thighs, and he rubs me over my sore pussy through my panties. "This makes you a whore, Summer. You put on this whole good girl act, but this shit right here—a paying customer's cum running out of your used-up cunt—makes you a fucking whore."

All I can do is sob as he rubs at my pussy. But unlike Lucca, who sets my body on fire, John makes me shut down. I feel like I'm going to pass out.

"You're out of the box," he says sharply. "I'll let you keep your fucking job because I know you need it and you've never messed up before, but the box is no longer available. You'll work the pole where I can watch your every move. Consider this probation."

More tears leak from my eyes.

"Unless," he utters, teasing his finger beneath the fabric.

I stiffen, terrified he'll stick his finger inside me. All he does is tease.

"Unless you wanted to work something out?" He smiles as he releases my throat and steps away.

Shaking my head sharply, I press my back farther against the door. "I-I won't do it again. I'm s-sorry. It was n-nothing."

His features darken. He's clearly pissed I don't

want to fuck him so he'll forgive me. I just want to get the hell out of here.

"The pole," he threatens.

The pole sure as hell beats *his* pole.

"I understand." I lift my chin and meet his evil stare. "The pole it is."

I step away from the door, and he storms out of the dressing room. Quickly, I pick up the money, then start throwing on my clothes, trying my hardest not to lose it to hysterics. My throat is tender, and I know it's going to bruise. And in that moment, I'm not thinking about how customers will see. Or how John might see them and feel bad. Or even how Lucca might see.

Tenderly, I touch my throat and sob.

I'm thinking of Christian and how he will see.

I'm so sorry.

7

Lucca

Everything about her was familiar, yet new.

Her taste—touch—scent. She's always been my weakness, and she proved tonight I'm hers. It's been six years, yet we still burn like wildfire.

Being inside her after so long was like coming home after a stint in the slammer.

Damn, I knew I missed her, though I wouldn't admit it out loud for so long, but fuck, I felt a relief I'm not comfortable analyzing when she kissed me back. And then, when she guided my cock inside her body, it felt like the six years had vanished and it was just us, like the time apart never happened.

The chemistry was electric and crackling between us—our bodies in sync, coming together like we were made to do so.

The shock in her eyes when I ripped off her mask excited me. Her finally seeing who'd been watching her all this time. Shock bled into need, and I fed that ache, gave her what she's been craving, missing all these years.

The past two days, all I've done is rehash how everything fell apart, but I did stop to think about her life now. Does she have someone in her life, a boyfriend...husband?

Fuck no. No way. Life wouldn't be that fucking cruel. It's dealt me enough blows already. The idea tonight was to talk to her to find out what the hell happened in her life to alter it so dramatically off course. But when she began dancing and stripped out of those panties, waving her ass and my tattoo at the glass, I nearly came undone. I had to be inside her. Feel her on my skin—on my breath—my cock. I've had her so many times before, but the memory wasn't enough in the moment.

Leaning against the side of the building, I wait for her to finish her shift. The idea of someone else watching her almost has me barging back in and tossing her over my shoulder like a caveman. She saves me from myself when she appears from a side door. Head down, oblivious to everything around her, she takes off running toward a beat up old car. It's the same one she had in college, a silver Honda. She named it Bubbles.

I don't see the same freedom on her face she used to have, though. There's worry and stress etched into her features.

As I approach her, she startles and holds her hands up as if to defend from an attack.

She pales, then sighs a relieved breath when she sees it's me. There's a lump and the starting of a bruise forming across her cheek. Black streaks smudge under her eyes from tear stains.

"What the fuck happened?" I demand.

Sniffling, she shakes her head. "*You* happened, Lucca. You fucking happened. And now I'll be working the pole instead of the box because of you," she snaps, tugging her jacket around herself to ward off the evening chill. "Why the hell did you come back here? To humiliate me? Watch me for God knows how long, then act all fucking crazy when I walk into the tattoo shop like you hadn't been creeping on me for months?"

Mixed emotions crash into me, battling for the steering wheel in this conversation, and my usual shitty attitude shows its ugly face. "I didn't know it was you. I can't fucking see your face in the box, Autumn—or is it Summer?" I sneer, looking her up and down with distaste. "I didn't come here to watch *you*, it was just a weird fucking coincidence."

"You expect me to believe that? Like you wouldn't recognize me because a mask covered some of my face, Lucca?"

"It's the fucking truth! Your body has changed in the past six years and this is the last place I'd ever expect to see you working, like some fucking whore." The slap comes fast. It rings my ears, burns a fire up my cheek. I deserved that.

"You don't ever get to call me a whore," she says, scarily calm.

The wad of cash I gave her in the box flutters around me like confetti as she yanks it from her purse and chucks it at me.

Grabbing her wrist, I stop her from throwing out any more. Her phone and lipstick have fallen to the ground, and she's crying, but it's not sorrowful tears, it's red-hot anger.

"I didn't mean to call you a whore, Breezy…" I implore.

"Don't call me that either. I haven't been her in a long ass time. You left, and she died when you did. My life was wrecked, and I had to pick up the pieces and do whatever I could to make it work."

"You're making no sense. What happened to your dream of becoming a teacher? How the fuck did you end up in here?"

Jerking her wrist from my grasp, she bends to snatch up her phone, shoving it back in her purse. Drunken idiots spill from the club, loud and obnoxious, making Autumn flinch and grab the lapels of her coat close around her again.

"I have to go, Lucca. You can be a dick to me another day, okay?"

Not okay. Not fucking okay.

I don't want to be a dick to her any day.

"What happened to your face? Did that club owner prick do that?"

Her bottom lip trembles. "Why do you care?"

"I never stopped caring, Breezy," I sigh out.

"Stop calling me that! I'm not her anymore," she barks, fumbling with her keys, trying to open her car.

"You'll always be her. It doesn't matter what name you give yourself or how much you think you've changed."

I watch her swallow the pain she's harboring as I track the tear that drops from her eye. I've seen her cry a million tears. She could create an ocean with the amount she's shed over me—us.

"I have to go," she whispers.

"Talk to me," I beg.

"I can't." She shakes her head, then opens her car door and slips inside, throwing her purse on the passenger side. She gazes at me for a couple silent beats, then ticks over the engine.

"Autumn, we need to fucking talk," I bite out, gaining attention from a couple girls smoking near the exit Autumn came from.

Her wheels kick up gravel as she peels out the car park, leaving me in a dust cloud. Fucking perfect. Sums my life up entirely. I pick up her discarded money and shove it in my pocket. I'll give this shit back to her the first chance I get. She clearly needs it more than I do.

I march over to the girls smoking, already knowing this is going to cost me. "Who bruised Summer's face?" I ask.

One of the girls shrugs, popping gum. Cliché as fuck.

"Who wants to know? Are you Christian?" She places a hand on her hip, giving me a once over.

Who the fuck's Christian?

"Shhh," the other one snaps, shoving her coworker with her shoulder.

I dig out a hundred dollar bill, hold it up between two fingers, and quirk a brow. The one who told the other to shush rolls her eyes before snatching it out of the air.

"The boss can be a bit hands-on, but he doesn't usually act that way with Summer. She's his flavor of the month."

"Who's Christian?" I ask.

She holds her hand out for more money. Growling, I dig out a fifty and slap it onto her palm. She shrugs, stuffing it in her bra. "Not sure. She mentions him to John like it's her man or something. A husband, perhaps, waiting at home for her."

My gut coils. Visions of her breathing my name tonight and coming undone over my cock assault me. I shake my head in disbelief. No way can there be a husband.

Jogging over to my car, I pull out of the parking lot, my head racing with the new information. She didn't have that bruise when I was fucking her. That cunt boss must have gotten handsy with her afterward. He's going to pay for putting his hands on my girl. *My girl.* No matter what her situation is, she will always be my girl. I have no clue where I'm going, or what direction she went in. I contemplate going back and fishing out more money for those girls in hopes they know where she lives, but like fucking fate is on my side for once, I see her car in a gas station across the street. I wait for her to get back in, then follow her. This isn't done between us, and I can't stew on shit another night wondering who the hell gets to take her home—who gets to love her like I used to—like I did tonight.

She's mine. She's fucking mine.

When she turns onto a back road, I kill my lights so she won't see she's being followed and panic over it being one of the dicks from the club. *It is a dick from the club.*

When she pulls into a driveway, I recognize the place straightaway—her mother's house. A white, beat-up wooden farmhouse with a wraparound porch and wind chimes hanging from every branch of the surrounding trees. *That noise used to drive her fucking crazy.*

I pull in behind her. She jumps out of the car, her expression startled as soon as she sees me. I frown. Her mother wasn't my biggest fan, but there's more fear on her face than warranted. She runs over to my car and tries to shove me back inside. "Get the hell outta here, stalker. I will meet you tomorrow. You *can't* be here."

"Why?" I snap. "Because of your husband, Christian?"

She looks surprised by my words and shakes her head manically. "How do you…? N-No, he's not my husband, Lucca."

"Then who the fuck is he? I'm done with dancing around everything. I need to know what the fuck happened to you. You gave up on me for this shit, Breezy?"

"No, I didn't give up on you. You seem to have memory confusion because it was you who fucked me, then threw me away. Told me I was nothing but a fuck. One you could replace easily enough."

Slamming my car door, I clasp onto her face, holding her cheeks between my palms. "That's a fucking lie, and you know it," I growl. "I bet my heart on you, and I lost! I offered you to come home with me. To help me. To love me. You told me no. I fucking loved you! Damn, I *still* love you, Breezy. I've never gotten you out of my system. Hell, I've been watching you for months, obsessed without even knowing it was you. You're ingrained in me. I seek you out in every woman. In everything."

She's sobbing, and I can't fucking stand to see her so distressed and broken.

I crash her to me, pinning her to my chest while running my hands through her hair and kissing her head. She grips my shirt, tugging and crying against me. It's so strangled and broken, my knees almost buckle from the weight of her pain.

The porch light suddenly turns on, blinding me, and her mother appears in her robe at the top of the steps.

"Autumn, honey, is that you?"

Pulling away from my hold, she swipes at her face and clears her throat. "Yes, Mother. I'll be right in."

"Christian is asking for you," her mother calls back, making me stiffen. There's that fucking name again.

"*Who* is Christian, Autumn?" I choke.

"Who is that with you?" her mother asks. The woman won't shut up.

"*Who* is Christian, Autumn?" I repeat.

Her sad, expressive eyes gaze up at me, and her lip trembles. And then, the world dims from focus when a small form joins her mother on the porch, and calls out, "Mommy?"

No…no way. Autumn holds her hand out to me as she backs away toward the house. I can't take my eyes from the young boy clinging to Autumn's mother's leg.

When she reaches the steps, she turns, transforming from broken dancer to beaming mother. "It's late, mister. Why are you still up?"

"I can't sleep," the boy tells her.

My insides swish around like I'm on a spin cycle. What the hell is happening?

"Who is that with you?" her mother asks.

"A friend. He followed me home after I was having car trouble to make sure I arrived safely. Now, please take Christian inside, Mother. It's late and cold." She ruffles the boy's hair. "I'll be in to read you a story in just a minute, sweetheart." She waits until they've gone back inside, then descends the steps and comes back over to me. I must look like a deer in the headlights because my jaw is unhinged and I can't form words.

She's a mom.

"You have a kid," I manage to choke out after a silent pause.

"Christian, yes. He's my son." She studies me, her arms crossed in a defensive way, her teeth nibbling away anxiously at her lip. My head fucking whirls, and I try to gauge his age and who she could have been with after me. "How old is he?"

Her chin wobbles, and her face crashes as she weakly offers, "Five."

Five.

Five.

She must have gotten pregnant with him almost immediately. She moved on and had a fucking kid while I was grieving not just my dad, but her—my life with her.

"You moved on real quick, huh? Couldn't give up school and move with me, but could go off and have a fucking kid with who? Who the fuck knocked you up and left you? Because he sure didn't stick around. Otherwise, why the hell are you living with your mom and working that ass to pay the bills!"

Damn, I'm angry. Distraught at the thought of her being pregnant with another man's baby. Sharing something so sacred with someone who isn't me. She's silent, gulping down tears and shaking her head at me with a furrowed brow.

"Who?" I bark. If it's someone I know, I'm going to lose my shit.

"He's…" She gags, then retches, doubling over and vomiting all over the ground. Oh my fucking God. Is she going to tell me something horrible? I can't fucking take this shit. It's all too much at once. Swiping a hand over her mouth, she rights herself, and says, "I'm sorry, Lucca."

"Sorry for what?" I laugh without humor. She's mumbling words, and I don't know what the fuck to say or think.

"For not telling you." She cradles herself and closes her eyes.

"Not telling me what?" I demand.

"He's your son," she blurts out, her lips trembling.

He's your son. He's your son. He's your son.

Air flees my lungs, and a buzzing noise invades my head. Her words rattle around on repeat, stabbing at me with sickness.

"What?" I breathe, dragging oxygen in to keep myself standing.

"That goodbye…the day your dad died and I came over…" she whispers, wringing her hands. "I didn't find out until I was four months along. Mom had had a minor stroke and lost her job, and you were so fucking cruel and angry when you left…"

"He's my son? You had my fucking kid?" I'm saying the words, but they feel foreign on my tongue and to my ears.

"Life changed so fast, and I was hit by a tidal wave. I was drowning. I am suffocating trying to stay afloat. Life got dark so fast, and I just needed to keep food on the table and the lights on. The club was just supposed to be temporary—easy money to see us through until I could save enough to move into our place and get a teaching position."

"He's my son?"

"Yes," she cries.

"Does he know?" I ask, dumbfounded at this turn of events. *A fucking dad. I'm a dad?* At her silence, I walk the distance between us and grab her upper arms, imploring her, "Does he know about me?" I repeat.

"Yes, of course." She nods frantically.

I'm a father. I collapse over her, hugging her to me. "You had my son. I have a son."

"We…we have a son, yes," she breathes into my chest, clinging to me.

"I need to meet him."

"Time, Lucca. In time."

Pulling her away from me, I grip her chin in my hand and look deep into her wild eyes.

"I've missed enough fucking time, Breezy. I want to meet my son. Now."

8

Breezy

Now?

Oh God.

"I...uh, I..." I trail off, choking on my words.

"I won't leave until I see him." His tone is fierce, but his eyes tenderly search mine, crumbling all the walls I've worked so hard to erect around my heart.

Christian is his son.

I've protected Christian from my work life, but I can't protect him from his own father. There's no need. Lucca may have broken my heart, but Christian is still his. He's not a danger to my son.

"Okay," I whisper. "He's sensitive and quiet. Not your typical rowdy boy. I...uh, it's just that it's late and sometimes he gets crabby."

He frowns. "You think I won't like my own kid?"

"N-No," I rush out. "I just worry. I don't want to hurt him."

"Everything's going to be okay."

The conviction behind his words has me taking his offered hand. For so long, I've done everything myself. I've assured myself everything is going to be okay. But I had to be the one to make that happen. Now that Lucca is here, making promises, it's hard to deny the pull he has on me.

He's quiet as we enter the dark house. The light is on in Christian's bedroom, and it pours into the hallway. I turn to Lucca before we make it to the doorway.

"Let me talk to him for a minute, okay?"

Lucca nods, his expression unreadable. I'm a bundle of nerves. I peek my head around the corner and find it's just Christian sitting on the bed with a book in his lap.

"Did Grandma go to bed?"

He nods. "Can you read a story, Mommy?"

"I can," I assure him. "And then I want you to meet someone."

His blue eyes widen and he perks up. "Your friend outside?"

"Yes," I whisper. "He's...uh, he's someone really special."

"Will he read me a story?"

The floorboard creaks, and I whip my head around. Lucca walks into the bedroom, a gentle smile on his handsome face. My heart aches at seeing them meet for the first time.

"I'm Lucca," Lucca says, kneeling beside the bed.

Christian jerks his head my way, silently asking, "My dad?"

"This is Lucca Russo," I confirm. "Your father."

I hold my breath. The room is so quiet, you could hear a pin drop.

"Can I call you Daddy?" Christian asks him.

Lucca turns to look at me, a wild mixture of happiness and awe on his face. "Can he?"

"Of course," I breathe, choking back tears.

Christian beams at me, then turns to Lucca. "Were you lost?"

Lucca's jaw clenches, and he lets out a heavy sigh. "Yeah, buddy, I was. Really lost."

"I think Mommy was sad you were lost," Christian tells him, his bottom lip poking out. "I was sad too."

Lucca shoots me a heartbroken look that stabs me right in the heart. He left me. I was knocked up with his son and all alone. I was scared—scared not only that he'd push me away again, but also push away his perfect little boy.

"Breezy," Lucca says, clearing his throat as he stands. "Why don't you take a shower and put your pajamas on? I'll read Christian a story."

"Breezy?" Christian asks.

Lucca kicks off his shoes and pulls off his jacket before gesturing for Christian to scoot to the middle of the bed. "You want me to read you this story or tell you how your mommy got the nickname Breezy?" Lucca winks at me to let me know he plans on making something up.

"Tell me the Breezy story!" Christian exclaims.

Lucca settles next to him, and they both look at me with matching grins. Same eyes. Same nose. Same smile. It's too much. Something I secretly dreamed about for years.

"I'm going to shower," I choke out. "Be right back."

I bolt from the room, needing a moment to collect myself. It isn't until I'm in the shower under the hot spray that I allow myself to feel all the emotions from the night. Sobs rattle through me, making my entire body tremble. I'm so tired. Not from the night, but from this life. I'd been barreling along, but recently ran out of steam, just coasting, praying I didn't sputter to a stop. Tonight, I feel like someone else has taken the driver's seat. It's hard to give up that control, though.

After spending way too much time in the shower, I quickly dry off and dress in some sweats and a T-shirt. I brush my teeth, eager to get the taste of vomit from my mouth, and stare at my reflection. Without the makeup I wear heavily for the club, I'm just me. Autumn. Christian's mom who's doing her best all by herself.

Not anymore.

The hopeful thought makes my gut churn. What if he leaves again? I don't let that bitterness linger and rush from the bathroom.

When I make my way back into Christian's room, he and Lucca are talking quietly. By the way Lucca furrows his brows, it's serious.

"Just in time," Lucca says, chasing the frown with a smile. "We were waiting for you to come back so we could read the story." He picks up the book. "But I can't read it. It's gibberish."

Christian giggles. "The book's upside down, silly."

"No way!" Lucca gasps in exaggeration. He flips the book around and laughs. "Well, looky there. I can read it now!"

Their laughter has about ten pounds worth of stress lifting from my shoulders. I crawl into the bed on the other side of Christian. I'm tired. I hurt everywhere, both inside and out. My emotions are a mess. As Lucca reads to Christian, I rake my fingers through my son's hair and snuggle him. One day, I'll have a job where I don't have to leave him at night and we can have lots of story time together. Lucca's voice is a relaxing timbre that lulls me to sleep.

•••••▬•••••

I wake with a start, confused in the darkened room. It takes a moment to realize I'm in my bed and the heavy arm wrapped around me belongs to Lucca. Being in bed with him has familiarity and longing thrumming through me.

"Christian?" I ask, my voice thick with sleep.

"He fell asleep and I brought you to bed."

I brought you to bed.

My body prickles with awareness. Everywhere he invades my space is on high alert. Hot breath against my damp hair. Large hand splayed over my stomach. Hard erection pressed against my ass.

"Autumn." My name on his lips is fierce, angry, betrayed.

"I'm sorry," I whisper. "You left and…I just couldn't bear for you to reject him too."

He's quiet for a moment. "I said shitty things I didn't mean, baby. I fucked up. I'm so sorry."

Words I never thought I would hear engulf me like a tidal wave. I'm swept under, drowning in them. Tears leak from my eyes. My body trembles. It's not unusual for me to break down in the dark. What is unusual is having someone hold me through it. Not just anyone, but him. Lucca Russo.

"I'm going to make things right," he vows, nuzzling my hair. "Let me make things right, Breezy."

Six years of being strong, and I just let go, let the tension bleed from my body as I exhale a deep breath. "Ok-kay."

Okay?

I'm really going to do this?

Nothing about the way he holds me and cuddles me feels wrong. Nothing about the way he looked so right beside Christian wearing a matching grin felt wrong. Everything feels unbelievably right with him warm beside me.

"I want to kiss you," he murmurs, pulling me down onto my back. In the dark, he moves the hair from my face gently, then presses kisses to my skin, lingering when he finds my lips. His leg slides between mine, and he tangles us together. Our kisses are sweet. We take our time, remembering how the other felt with soft brushes and swipes of the tongue. When he playfully tugs at my bottom lip with his teeth, I let out a breathy chuckle.

"There she is," he murmurs. "There's the girl I've missed every day for six years."

"I missed you too," I admit. "I never could bear to date anyone. It just didn't feel right because I had Christian to take care of."

He presses a kiss to my nose. "I didn't see anyone either. I was so fucking angry and depressed over losing you. No one compared, Breezy. No one. I took care of my sister the best I could, dealt with the bar, then came home each night and jacked off to memories of us." He lets out a heavy sigh. "It fucked me in the head. I never cared to participate with anyone because they weren't you. That's why

I was into that bullshit I did at the club. Watching. Pretending. But never doing. I never could move on."

His words are like a dam breaking in my heart. All the love we made together comes flooding back inside me. The rush is like nothing I've ever felt before. Suddenly, our clothes feel like too much. I need him. I just need him.

He all but rips my clothes off me. His follow quickly behind. Then, his hot body is on mine, his mouth urgent and insistent. I moan, accepting him in every way. Our tongues lash as he spreads me open and pushes into me, so feral, so needy, my back arches off the bed. I'm still not used to his piercings, but I'm growing to quickly love the way they massage all the tender spots inside me.

God, I've missed him so much.

It's like all the times before, but better. Absence makes the heart grow fonder. I appreciate every thrust of his hips, each swirl of his tongue against mine, every single groan that vibrates from him. I memorize the moment because I realize moments can be stolen from us. I cling to him, conveying how much I need him and can't lose him again. His intensity ripples as he makes silent vows with his body.

The pleasure builds and builds within me. When he touches my clit, I finally tumble off the cliff. My cry of ecstasy is silenced by his deep kiss. I clench around him with each shudder of my orgasm until I milk his own release from him. Heat floods inside me.

Careless, hopeless, dumb fools.

With Lucca, I lose all sense of reality.

Women with no sex lives don't need birth control. And men with no sex lives clearly forget to put on a rubber. The fact that we keep sleeping together so irresponsibly should mess me up in the head, but I can't help but relax in his arms.

He doesn't pull out of me despite the fact that he's softened and his cum leaks out onto the bed. It's as though he misses our closeness every bit as much as I do.

"Breezy, I love you. I never stopped."

My heart stutters in my chest. "I can't lose you again. I just can't, Lucca. My heart won't survive it."

"You won't," he growls. "I'm here. I'm not going anywhere. We're a family."

I choke out a loud, ugly sob. A family. It feels too good to be true. He kisses me until I calm back down.

"I swear to God, Breezy, I'm going to make it all up to you. Let me love you and our son. We were always meant to be together. It's been proven. We're back here together, and you had my son. I can't lose out on any more time with him or you."

"I love you too," I whisper. "I never stopped, even when it hurt so bad. Seeing Christian every day was nothing but a reminder of how much I love you." I playfully swat his shoulder. "But keep screwing me without a rubber and you're going to expand this family whether you want to or not." I won't lie and say giving Christian a sibling isn't something I've always wanted.

His cock thickens inside me. "I'm making up for lost time, baby."

And with those words, he thrusts into me hard enough, the bed bangs against the wall. I dig my fingernails into his biceps and kiss him as deeply as I can. I want to make up for lost time too.

A future without Lucca isn't one I wanted, but was given anyway.

I hold on tight so it never happens again.

He's mine, and I'm not letting go.

9

Lucca

Life has a way of doing a one-eighty on you when you least expect it. Damn, my head is still spinning.

Last time it happened, my world shattered, and I made sacrifices thinking I was doing the right thing. I don't regret going home to raise Sofina. My baby sister needed me, and I'll always be there to take care of her, but it was at a hefty price.

Her. Him. My other family.

Missing out on Breezy's pregnancy and five years of my son's life hurts. I have a lot of time to make up for, and I intend to do that. Give him everything he deserves and more. I've learned time is precious and can change in a heartbeat, so as soon as possible, I'm taking my girl down the aisle—putting a ring on her finger and making this family official.

"Well, it took longer than I expected, but I knew you'd be back," Autumn's mother Judy says, shuffling into the kitchen and taking a seat at the breakfast table.

I took the liberty of making a feast for everyone. I'm not missing another meal with my kid. Autumn was worn out after I kept her up all night, so I reluctantly slipped out of bed and got acquainted with the kitchen.

"I would have been back sooner had I known," I state firmly, serving her some eggs, then taking the seat next to her.

"She was broken when you left," Judy says with a frown. "I think it helped her to be angry and have someone else to focus on. Christian changed her. Changed us both."

"He's already changing me. I'm not going anywhere ever again. I'm going to speak to Autumn—"

"Speak to Autumn about what?" Autumn interrupts me, coming to kiss her mother on the head and taking the seat on the other side of me.

Clearing my throat, I push my coffee mug in her direction and turn my chair slightly to face her. "I don't want you working at that club," I say, checking her face for signs she's pissed.

Sipping my drink, she flits her eyes to her mother, then back to me. "It's not ideal, but it's how I make enough money to pay the bills."

"It's not safe, baby. That motherfucker put his hands on you and will only make your life harder. There's no way you're going out on that pole, Breezy. You did what you had to, but I'm here now, and I'm going to take care of you all."

"Lucca," she whispers, frowning.

"I have quite a bit of savings from the sale of the bar and a job that will see us through. You can finally do what you've always wanted and become a teacher."

"Morning, Daddy," Christian chirps from the doorway, taking off running and launching himself at me. My heart nearly explodes in my chest. Insta-love is a real fucking thing. It's madness. I didn't even know this kid existed less than twenty-four hours ago, and now I'd give my life for his—take on the whole fucking world for him.

"I'm chopped liver now," Autumn snorts, stealing my bacon.

I hug my son and grin over at my girl. This is what happiness must fucking feel like.

"I'm with Lucca, by the way. If you want my opinion." Judy shrugs, pushing her eggs around her plate.

"My boss won't take it well," Autumn says, chewing her lip.

I beam down at our son. She's not going to fight me on this. "I'll inform him. You don't ever have to see him again," I tell her, tickling Christian's tummy when he looks up at me in wonder.

His giggles fill the room, and I see a tear build and leak from my girl's eye.

"Christian, come, let Grandma get you dressed," Judy says after we finish our meal. "Then you can help me in the garden while Mommy and Daddy talk."

Once they leave the room, I drag Autumn into my lap and swipe her tears away with the pads of my thumbs. They just keep coming. So many tears, but at least they're happy ones. "This is the start of our new life, Breezy. I don't want to see any more tears in your eyes."

"They're happy tears." She sniffles. "I feel so happy. I'm terrified I'm going to wake up and find out it's all a dream."

Grasping her cheeks, I kiss her deep and long, until she's gasping for air. "This is a dream. We're living the fucking dream, baby."

Walking into the club in the middle of the day casts a whole new light on the place. The girls dancing on the poles look half-assed and bored. The bartender I usually deal with is replaced with a badly aged woman, fake tits far too many sizes bigger than her frame. Wrinkles like a road map litter her face, showing signs of a hard life. "What can I get you, darling?" she asks, sugary sweet.

"I need to see the boss," I tell her.

"If you have a complaint, you can leave a comment card and we'll be sure to get to it." She snorts, narrowing her eyes at me.

Speak of the damn devil. The smug, woman-beating prick saunters from the back room reading something on his phone.

Giving the bartender the finger, I march over to him. When he looks up, I jut my head forward, connecting with his nose, relishing in the crunch.

He stumbles backward, his phone dropping to the floor and blood pissing from his nostrils like I turned on a tap. "Motherfucker," he sputters, cupping his face.

I eye two bouncers heading my way, so I act quickly, lifting my leg and booting the bastard in the balls. When he doubles over, I bring my knee up to connect with his face. He lands on the floor in a heap just as I'm grabbed from behind.

"Summer fucking quits, prick," I snap.

I'm dragged through the club and thrown into the bright light of day out the side door. I land with a thud, the asphalt scraping my hands.

"You're banned," the biggest fucker barks.

"I have the real deal at home, assholes." I smirk, taking the immediate kick to my gut like a champ.

Coughing up my insides, I wrap a hand around my stomach and get to my feet.

This place is in the rearview for us both.

Driving back to Autumn's, I feel like I have a new lease on life. I pull up her driveway, elated to find them both already on the porch waiting for me. My woman and my boy. I watch in wonder as they bound down the steps toward the car, jumping inside to see me.

The future starts now.

Autumn blasts the radio, and Christian settles into the booster seat I bought as soon as I left them this morning.

A familiar voice croons from the speakers, and Christian cheers. "Turn it up, Daddy. Mommy said this is my aunty singing on the radio."

Grinning like a fool over at my woman, I look back at Christian and nod. "It sure is, buddy, and she's going to love you so much. We can go visit her during your summer break from school if Mommy says it's okay."

"Can we, Mommy? Pleaaaseee."

"Sure thing, baby. It's more than okay. She's our family too, and I'm learning that's the most important thing in the world." Autumn reaches over and squeezes my hand. Before she can pull away, I clutch onto it and curl my fingers around hers. I'm never letting it go ever again.

Turning the radio up, I look in the rearview mirror at Christian and blurt the lyrics with him as I pull out of the drive.

Hold me. Love me.
Please…just take care of me.
And I'll take care of you too.

Sofina's voice filters through the speakers, and for the first time in a long time, I feel at home. Happy. Complete.

No more watching, just fucking living.

EPILOGUE

Breezy

Three months later...

"Don't touch that," I whisper to Christian. "In fact, don't touch anything."

Lucca laughs at my hovering. "Kids will be kids. Trust me, Ronan can afford to replace a glass candy dish."

I purse my lips, and he simply grins at me. That man always gets his way when he smiles. My man. It's hard to believe it's true. Three months ago, he stormed into my life, made his presence known to our son, and has upheld his promise to love and take care of us. Every damn day, he proves what an amazing man he is. He makes up for lost time. My heart breaks at all the years we lost, but we're not wasting another second.

"Come on," Lucca says, grabbing Christian's hand. "Aunt Sofina said she'd be in a recording room working on some lyrics."

Aunt Sofina.

I still can't believe I have a sister-in-law. When I glance down at the diamond wedding ring on my finger, I let out a happy sigh. We've been married less than a month, and I still stare at the ring in awe sometimes.

Sofina's surely changed. She's no longer the little girl Lucca ran off to raise. Sofina grew up well—thanks to her amazing big brother—and is conquering the world one chart-smashing track at a time. Her music is incredible. It's all Christian and I listen to when we're in the car together. We're proud, that's for certain.

And Sofina's pretty pleased with her little nephew too. I guess when you're a self-made millionaire at such a young age, you have no qualms throwing money at whatever makes you happy. In Sofina's case, she bought her brother a house with the most wonderful playroom for Christian. At first, Lucca balked because my man is as proud as they come, but she reminded him he once gave up his entire life to make sure she was taken care of. Her buying him a house for her adorable little nephew was the least she could do to show her appreciation.

I love the house, but I love who lives inside it more.

As if cued into my thoughts, my husband casts a glance over his shoulder, heating me to my core with one fiery look. Sometimes, I barely make it to my teacher certification program classes because he burns me alive with his sexy glares. When I give in and finally allow him to ravish me, he simply grins and pats my ass before telling me to have a good night. It'd be infuriating, but it's everything I've always wanted. Finishing my degree while he was gone and my heart was broken was difficult. When I walked away with my Bachelor's in education, I felt proud, but I didn't have the energy to finish what I needed to move on to the next stage of becoming a teacher. Plus, Mom had her stroke and Christian was an infant. I was needed on the home front. Now that I don't have to work and Lucca looks after Christian in the evenings, I'm able to finally finish what I started.

We make it to the elevator, and Ronan stalks out

of it, his face contorted in fury. Lucca frowns at him as he tucks Christian close to him in a protective way that makes my heart flutter. Ronan charges past where we came in at the same time someone bursts in the door.

"I told you the next time you showed up here I was calling the cops," Ronan bellows, facing off with the man.

Not just any man.

Oh my God.

"Xavi Jacobs," Lucca hisses in shock. "That's Xavi Jacobs from Berlin Scandal."

Holy crap.

Xavi is the lead singer of Lucca's favorite band. Tall, lean but muscular, a face of a broken angel. Beautiful, yet tragically broken. But Xavi is a media nightmare. Always getting trashed in public and making a scene. He looks drunk and pissed off. Not a good combination.

"You need to go," Ronan barks. "We have gone over this a thousand times. You can't keep showing up."

"Fuck you, Ronan Hayes. Fuck you and your label." Xavi kicks the table with the candy dish, and it hits the floor, shattering.

Christian's mouth pops open. "Mommy, he broke it!"

"Shhh," I whisper.

Xavi's fury melts momentarily when he blinks our way, taking in the fact that a family is watching him lose his shit. Shame washes over his features. But before he has a chance to bolt, a cop storms in. Not just a regular cop, but a big-ass scary hot cop. His muscles bulge as he charges over to Xavi.

Xavi looks like he wants to flip out, but again, he casts a look our way. It's apologetic almost. Lost. My heart breaks for him. I hope he and Ronan can sort it out. The cop grips Xavi's bicep in a punishing hold and all but drags him away. The three of them walk into an empty office, and the door closes behind them.

"Awkward," Lucca grumbles, ruffling his son's hair. "Let's go see your aunt."

Lucca

One month later...

I stare at my sleeping son—fuck, that never gets old—a moment longer before closing the door. When I pad down the hallway, I shake my head. I can't believe Sofina bought me a damn house. I wanted to be pissed, but she's sassy now that she's with Ronan and singing for the whole fucking world. She told me to shut up and deal with it. Actually, her words were, *"You need to stop being a prideful asshole. It's for my nephew. You took care of me when you didn't have to, and I never really told you how much I appreciated you for that and love you. Now, let me take care of you a little, big bro."* How was I supposed to argue with that?

But this house is a home because of Breezy. She's an incredible decorator and has worked hard to pull in as many family pictures as she can into her décor. Sometimes, I stand in front of the fireplace for hours staring at our wedding picture. It was a small wedding on a lake nearby. A few close friends and family. I love the picture because

Christian hangs from my back like a monkey while I kiss his mom. It's so fucking adorable.

I step into our room and hear the shower going. A thrill shoots through me knowing Breezy is back from her class. I have good news to tell her, and I can't wait to kiss her dizzy before laying it on her. We had to go through hell for six years to find our heaven. But, fuck, is it ever heaven now.

Locking the door behind me—I've learned my damn lesson after one too many times of our son walking in on us—I strip out of my clothes on the way to the bathroom. Once inside the fancy bathroom, I sit in the chair Breezy always uses to put on her makeup. The bathroom is steamy, but I can see her form beyond the glass. Lazily, I grip my dick and stroke it as I watch her from across the room.

The moment she senses me, she turns and steps close to the door. She writes *I love you* in the glass, then begins a seductive, teasing dance as she soaps her body down. Her hand swipes through the steam, giving me a clear view of her perfect body.

Standing, I continue to jerk at my dick as I watch her rinse off. Once I'm close enough, my dick nearly touching the glass, she bats her long lashes at me in a coy way that drives me mad with need.

"Touch yourself, Breezy," I rumble, stroking myself slowly.

She flutters her fingertips over her hard nipple. "Here?"

I shake my head. "Lower, baby."

Her hand skims down over her stomach to her pussy. "Here?"

"Mmhmm. Touch your clit."

Our eyes lock as she teases her clit. I'm reminded of those times when she unknowingly danced for me inside that glass box. Difference is, now she's all mine and I never have to share her again.

"Put your foot on the seat," I order. "Show me how pink and needy your cunt is."

A small gasp escapes her at my words, but my girl obeys. She slides her fingers between her pussy lips and opens them so I can see her clit that practically throbs to be sucked on.

"Are you juicy for my cock, wife?" I growl.

Her finger slides into her heat, and she nods. "So wet."

Unable to keep up the game any longer, I fling

open the glass and prowl into the steam after her. As soon as my hands find her hips, she practically launches herself at me, attacking my mouth with hers. I grip her ass, lifting her light body and impaling her on my cock. Her moan is music to my damn ears. Leaning her against the tile, I drive into her over and over again, claiming this gorgeous woman as mine.

"Lucca," she moans. "Oh God."

"Tell me what I want to hear, Breezy. Scream it."

"I love you!"

Damn right.

Sucking on her bottom lip, I reach between us to give her clit a few firm circles, taking her right to the edge where she belongs. I whisper that I love her too and pinch her clit just right. My girl orgasms long and hard until she milks my own release from me. I thrust a few more times until I'm spent and drained. Our kisses become sweet and adoring.

"I have good news, Mrs. Russo," I tell her, pulling away slightly so I can see her face.

"Me too, Mr. Russo." She tugs her lip between her teeth in a way that has my cock jolting despite just coming inside her.

"You first."

"Nope, this is your show," she says with a smile. "I'll tell you mine after."

"Jake's expanding. He wants to open a new shop next year."

Her brows pinch together. "Are you leaving?"

"Never again, baby. Never again." I lean my forehead against hers. "Jake's going to leave to go launch that one, but he needs someone responsible and capable to manage this shop. By then, I'll be a full-time artist. He said if all goes well, he'll give me the option to buy it from him. With the money from the sale of Dad's bar to Sofina and my bar owning experience, I think I can do this. I want to do this."

"I know you can do this," she assures me. "You're the most amazing man I know."

We kiss again until she's breathless. I pull away, and her whine makes me chuckle.

"You can sex me up later, Breezy. What's your news?"

"I may need to put off my teaching job for another year." Her eyes are bright and twinkling. "Another opportunity—one I've wanted for a while—has come along."

"What is it?"

She looks down between us. "Our recklessness has caught up with us again." Her smile makes my heart squeeze in my chest.

"No," I choke out. "No fucking way."

"You have super sperm," she sasses.

I laugh and kiss her hard. "You're kidding me. I'm going to be a daddy again? Christian is going to have a sibling?"

Holy fucking shit.

She nods, tears welling in her eyes. "Are you happy?"

"I'm fucking over the moon, baby. We're going to have another baby!"

I'm hard and eager to celebrate the best news ever. I fuck my wife until the water grows icy cold, then carry her out of the shower while she's still on my dick. Just before she comes, I slide her off my dick and flip her around to face the mirror. I grip a handful of her dark hair and bend her over the counter.

"Watch me, Breezy. Watch me fuck you. I want you to see what I see every damn day. The most beautiful woman in the world. My woman. The best mother ever. Gorgeous as fuck. I love you so much, it fucking hurts sometimes." I push my cock back into her hot body, loving the way her eyes flutter closed. "Open them, wife."

Her eyes pop open and she watches me as I fuck her hard. Full tits that seem even bigger than usual bounce wildly as I own her wet body. Soon, she'll swell with my child and make me impossibly happier. From this angle, I am able to bring her to climax quickly as my dick hits her G-spot, turning her into a madwoman. Each one of my piercings rubs against her, two of them rotating on hitting the most sensitive spot with each thrust. She cries out and comes hard, drawing my own climax from me. Once we're wrung out, I slide out of her and set to drying off my shivering woman.

She dresses in a pair of my sweats and one of my hoodies, making my inner caveman growl like a fucking beast. I throw on a pair of gym shorts. We don't even make it to the bed before I'm kissing her again in a claiming way. Now that she's pregnant, I don't want her to walk anywhere. I'll just carry her to all the places.

A sweet squeal escapes her when I grab her ass and lift her. Her long legs wrap around my waist and her fingers thread together at the base of my neck.

"I love you," she breathes, grinning. "I don't think you can make me any happier than I am right now."

I bite at her bottom lip and smile back. "Watch me, baby. I'm only getting started."

The End

Up Next!

*From international bestselling authors, **Ker Dukey** and **K Webster** comes a **fast-paced**, hot, **MM** instalove **standalone** lunchtime read from their KKinky Reads collection!*

I got my dream from a young age.
The lead singer of one of the most popular bands in the world—Berlin Scandal.
I'm a rock god.
But underneath the façade of living the dream is dark secret consuming me.

Angry lyrics and a brooding attitude propelled my career.
Getting wasted and lashing out behind the scenes could be my downfall.
I'm spiraling and don't know how to stop the descent.

Now my record label has issued me a babysitter.
Blaine Mannford, a hardass detective with a dark thirst.
And he's looking at me like I can quench it.

He's not my type in more ways than one.
Bossy. Forceful. Firm. A man.
I don't like cops and I don't like him.

Unfortunately, he likes it when I fight him—enjoys punishing me how he sees fit.
I'm screwed up in the head, because I'm a willing player in his dirty game.
I want him to hurt me.

This is a steamy, kinky romance sure to make you blush! A perfect combination of sexy and intense you can devour in one sitting!

You'll get a happy ending that'll make you swoon!! **BOOKS**

BY
KER DUKEY & K WEBSTER

Pretty Little Dolls Series:
Pretty Stolen Dolls
Pretty Lost Dolls
Pretty New Doll
Pretty Broken Dolls

The V Games Series:
Vlad
Ven
Vas

KKinky Reads Collection:
Share Me
Choke Me
Daddy Me
Watch Me

The Elite Seven Series:
Lust by Ker Dukey
Pride by J.D. Hollyfield
Wrath by Claire C. Riley
Envy by MN Forgy
Gluttony by K Webster
Sloth by Giana Darling
Greed by Ker Dukey and K Webster

Four Fathers Series:
Blackstone by J.D. Hollyfield
Kingston by Dani Rene
Pearson by K Webster
Wheeler by Ker Dukey

Four Sons Series:
Nixon by Ker Dukey
Hayden by J.D. Hollfield
Brock by Dani Rene
Camden by K Webster

ACKNOWLEDGEMENTS

Thank you to our hottie husbands. Baby Daddy and Mr. Webster are the real inspirations!

Ker and K would like to thank each other for being so amazing and beautiful and sweet and precious and funny and talented and hard working and… yeah, you get the point. (We love each other 1000%!)

A huge thank you to our reader groups. You all are insanely supportive and we can't thank you enough.

Thanks so much to Terrie Arasin and Misty Walker! Two of the best PAs everrrr! We love you ladies!

A gigantic thank you to those who always help K out. Elizabeth Clinton, Ella Stewart, Misty Walker, Holly Sparks, Jillian Ruize, Gina Behrends, Wendy Rinebold and Nikki Ash—you ladies are amazing!

Great thanks to Ker's awesome ladies for helping make this book is as awesome as can be! Couldn't have done it without you: Ashley Cestra, Rosa Saucedo, PA Allison, Teresa Nicholson, and KimBookJunkie.

A big thank you to our author friends who have given us your friendship and your support. You have no idea how much that means to us.

Thank you to all of our blogger friends both big and small that go above and beyond to always share our stuff. You all rock! #AllBlogsMatter

Monica with Word Nerd Editing, thank you SO much for editing this book. You rock!!

Thank you Stacey Blake for being amazing as always when formatting our books and in general. We love you!

Lastly but certainly not least of all, thank you to all of the wonderful readers out there who are willing to hear our stories and enjoy the characters like we do. It means the world to us!

ABOUT
KER DUKEY

My books all tend to be darker romance, the edge of your seat, angst-filled reads. My advice to my readers when starting one of my titles… prepare for the unexpected.

I have always had a passion for storytelling, whether it be through lyrics or bedtime stories with my sisters growing up.

My mom would always have a book in her hand when I was young and passed on her love for reading, inspiring me to venture into writing my own. Not all love stories are made from light- some are created in darkness but are just as powerful and worth telling.

When I'm not lost in the world of characters, I love spending time with my family. I'm a mom and that comes first in my life, but when I do get down time, I love attending music concerts or reading events with my younger sister.

News Letter sign up: eepurl.com/OpJxT

Website: authorkerdukey.com

Facebook: www.facebook.com/KerDukeyauthor

Twitter: twitter.com/KerDukeyauthor

Instagram: www.instagram.com/kerdukey

BookBub: www.bookbub.com/profile/ker-dukey

Goodreads: www.goodreads.com/author/show/7313508.Ker_Dukey

Contact me here:
Ker: Kerryduke34@gmail.com
Ker's PA: terriesin@gmail.com

ABOUT
K WEBSTER

K Webster is the *USA Today* bestselling author of over seventy-five romance books in many different genres including contemporary romance, historical romance, paranormal romance, dark romance, sci-fi romance, romantic suspense, taboo romance, and erotic romance. When not spending time with her hilarious and handsome husband and two adorable children, she's active on social media connecting with her readers.

Her other passions besides writing include reading and graphic design. K can always be found in front of her computer chasing her next idea and taking action. She looks forward to the day when she will see one of her titles on the big screen.

Join K Webster's newsletter to receive a couple of updates a month on new releases and exclusive content. To join, all you need to do is go here (www.authorkwebster.com).

Facebook: www.facebook.com/authorkwebster

Blog: authorkwebster.wordpress.com

Twitter: twitter.com/KristiWebster

Email: kristi@authorkwebster.com

Goodreads: www.goodreads.com/user/show/10439773-k-webster

Instagram: instagram.com/kristiwebster

KKINKY READS
COLLECTION

They have one job.

Keep me safe.

But none of us are safe against the allure we have when we're together.

Control and professionalism used to be something they prided themselves on.

But now that we're secluded and alone, lines blur and control quickly loses to need.

Someone is trying to snuff out my life, but they may not get the chance if I'm devoured whole by my saviors first.

This is a fiery-hot mfmmm romance sure to make you self-combust! A perfect combination of sweet and sexy with a smidgen of suspense! You'll get a happy ending that'll make you swoon!

CHOKE Me

I had a plan.
Make Ren Hayes pay.
But plans don't always turn out the way we want them to.

He was found not guilty of murdering my best friend.
But that doesn't make him innocent.
In my eyes, he's guilty.

Guilty of charming everyone around him into believing his innocence.
Guilty of being so intoxicating I forget who he is—what he is.
And guilty of awakening parts of me I never knew existed before his touch.

I know eventually, I'll succumb.
His allure beckons me.
Keeping me on the edge of madness between lust and hate.

In the end, it's me who's guilty.
Guilty of allowing him to take my breath away.

This is a super steamy romance sure to take your breath away! A perfect combination of sweet and sexy with a smidgen of suspense that you can gobble up in just an hour or two! You'll get a happy ending that'll make you swoon!

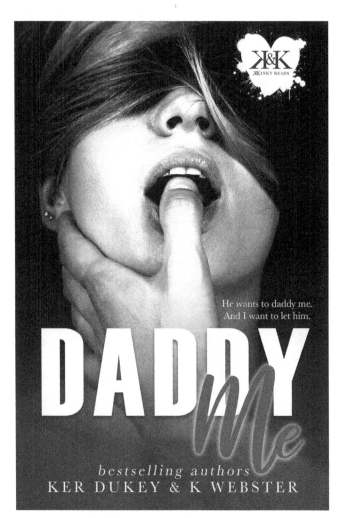

DADDY *Me*

Dreams are supposed to be encouraged.
Not mine.
My brother likes to keep me on a tight leash, tethered to an unexceptional life.
But when Ronan Hayes walks into our family-owned bar, he opens my cage and offers me freedom.

Ronan wants to give me the world.
A chance to take flight and soar.
He sees something special in me, and I want nothing more than to be that for him.
Special.

He's my dream maker.
My shot. My hope. My everything.

Ronan craves to take care of me.
A protector. A confidant. A provider. A lover.
He wants to daddy me.
And I want to let him.

Made in the
USA
Middletown, DE